WILD

HEAT

WILDING PACK WOLVES 3

ALISA WOODS

February 2016 Edition
Sworn Secrets Publishing

Cover Design by Steven Novak

ISBN-13: 978-1532729584
ISBN-10: 1532729588

Wild Heat (Wilding Pack Wolves 3)

**He's a hot cop. She's a wild artist.
Making art has never been so dangerously SEXY.**

Kaden Grant is well aware that the Seattle Police Department is no friend of
shifters. But when the mayor's favorite artist is targeted by the local hate-
fanatic, he orders protective custody for her… and Kaden is desperate to
land the assignment. Because any other cop would just get the girl killed. If
only her wild streak didn't threaten to bring out his long-buried secret…

Terra Wilding's family is being torn apart, and now the Wolf Hunter is
targeting her because her of photographs bringing out the light in the dark
corners of Seattle. The only way to keep her baby sister Cassie and the other
wolves safe is to leave her mountain refuge and hole up in a small house that
feels more like a cage. If only the human cop who's guarding her wasn't so
hot…

When Terra slips away to meet up with a secretive art collector, Kaden's
protective side goes into overdrive. He's an alpha's alpha, and he lights a
wild heat in her that threatens to burn them both down. Kaden wants
to *protect* and *serve,* but can he tame the wildest Wilding before the Wolf
Hunter catches up to them both?

CHAPTER 1

Terra Wilding's room was drenched in demonic light. It was merely the darkroom lamp bathing everything in its blood-red glow, but somehow, it fit the dark and haunted mood that had grabbed hold of her. Terra's new top-of-the-line enlarger had just shipped in, and she'd been itching to try it out, but all she had to work with were old shoots. Old film. Photographs that were taken months, if not even more stale. Her last gallery exhibition was eight weeks ago, and even that work had been shot months prior to that. It had been *so* long since she'd been able to scour the city—Seattle's people and buildings and grimy corners—to find some bit of life for her art. Some tiny shred of goodness that she could bring out to say to her hometown, *See, all is not lost, even in your days of hatred.*

With the multiple attacks on shifters recently, she wondered if that was still true.

She swished the photo paper in the developer until the images came up, rising out of the red darkness to reveal themselves. But there were no surprises. No new angle or viewpoint, no matter how much she cropped or sifted through her old shoots. She used the tongs to pull the print from the developer and slide it into the tray of stop solution. She simply needed new material—and she wasn't going to get it here at the River pack's safehouse, tucked up in the mountains, far from the heartbeats of the city.

Only her city wasn't safe for her anymore.

She moved the print to the fixer solution, then rinsed it in the final bath and hung the newly developed sheet on her clothesline. A heavy sigh escaped her as she gazed at the line of prints covering her wall—four rows high, twenty pictures long, covering two of the four walls with completely useless art. The third wall, the one with the window, had been swathed in light-blocking fabric as soon as she had arrived—two shades, a heavy set of curtains, and black tape around the edges. The fourth wall was taken up by the massive four-postered bed and some artwork that Terra couldn't remove because it would insult her hosts. They weren't half bad, actually— the art, not the hosts, who were wondrous. The paintings were realistic renderings of the gorgeous mountains that surrounded the safehouse ranch, but they weren't exactly her style. They itched at her, day after day, like a tag left in her shirt.

She sighed again, looking back at her own work, and gave up on trying to wrench anything meaningful out of it. Instead, she just switched on the main light for her room, slipped her sketchpad out of her nightstand and curled up on the bed.

During her endless internment at the safehouse, her need to create something new had returned her to an original love—drawing. But what kept rising out of the charcoal lines on her sketchpad was even darker than the things she captured with her camera lens—bombs, body parts, the blown-apart carnage of shifters and metal, cars and buildings reduced to their elemental parts by the hate group that was stalking the sprawling Wilding pack. The bombers weren't after *her* specifically, but she was one of the more visible members of her pack, what with her gallery showings and articles in *Artist Today*. The Wolf Hunter had outed her entire family as shifters in his doxing video, revealing all of their names and addresses, and the random haters in her city were all too eager to work out their dark mental issues in shifter blood and mayhem.

She would never understand the hatred and violence, but she understood the dark mental issues all too well. The darkness of the world had always sought her, closed in around her, threatened to drown her… and now, with the haters on the rise, it was getting harder to find the light that marched side-by-side with the dark.

She sighed again. She had been cooped up *too damn long*.

Terra closed her eyes and tried to imagine the soft innocence of her younger sister, Cassie. She'd always been a perpetual source of light in Terra's life, ever since their mom died. Cassie was a full-time resident at the safehouse too, and even Terra's twin brother, Trent, was becoming a more frequent visitor, tearing himself away from his frenetic work schedule at his software development company. Their father still puttered around in his estate in Bellevue, oblivious to everything, per usual. He probably hadn't even seen the bombings on the news. Terra often retreated into her world of art, but her father was the king of withdrawing from the real world—when her mother died, her father moved to Planet Donnie Wilding and never came back.

Terra rubbed her eyes and worked the tension from her shoulders. There was no point in dwelling on things that would never change. A knock at the door kept her from diving back into her drawing of Cassie.

"Come in!" Terra shouted.

Her cousin Noah swung open the door. He was about her age, twenty-one or two, but he'd been through a lot—far more than Terra. Just having him around reminded her of that. But lately, he'd been even more intimately involved in trying to stop the bombings… including the one that happened just this morning.

But his frown was unexpected, along with the harried, uncertain look on his face. "Terra, someone's at the door for you."

"Yeah?" She looked back to her drawing. "Really not interested right now, Noah."

"You need to come down."

She looked up.

His face had way too much deadly urgency. It sent a chill wind through her.

"Something's happened," he said.

Oh God, not again. Terra felt the darkness closing in like a wet wool blanket threatening to smother her. Sometimes she could feel the evil let loose in the world like it was an actual physical force, pressing on her body.

"All right." She opened the drawer in her nightstand and tucked her pad and pencil away.

Noah waited for her at the door, apparently wanting to escort her to make sure she complied.

Terra smoothed down her black t-shirt—it was stained with developing fluids. "I hope it's not the Queen of England."

"It's not." Noah didn't even crack a smile.

She frowned as she passed him in the doorway, and he followed her out into the hall. The Riverwise country estate was massive, and they had at least a little bit of time to wind through the corridors before they would get to wherever they were going—it looked like they were headed toward the front door.

"What's going on?" she asked.

"There's a new video from the Wolf Hunter." Noah

pressed his lips together and seemed hesitant to go on.

"And?" The sense of darkness squeezed on her chest. She could feel its presence in the words Noah didn't want to speak.

"And he's targeting you now, Terra." He seemed to have to force out the words.

Tara stopped in her tracks and held onto the pristine white wall. *"Me?"* The Wolf Hunter's first video had outed them all. Then a random series of videos gave voice to all his hate for shifters—a manifesto on film for his hate group followers. Then they assassinated her uncle—Arthur Wilding, one of the five Wilding brothers that lead the pack families—and targeted his daughter, Nova. Then her cousin Noah had come back from Afghanistan to help and nearly paid for it with his life. One by one, each of the families was being targeted, tested, hunted...

It must be her turn.

The floor seemed to sway under her feet.

"Terra, it's going to be all right." Her cousin's hand landed on the bare skin of her arm and helped hold her up.

"No, it's not." She shook off his hand, and he pulled back. The only armor she had against the overwhelming darkness—the hate and the terror pointed at her family like a weapon—was a deep well of rage. She put on that armor and pushed past Noah to march down the hallway. "Let's go."

The anger was invigorating. How *dare* this Wolf Hunter threaten her and her family? She hurried toward the front and whatever awaited her. As Noah hustled to catch up, her strides got longer, and her heavy black boots pounded the polished wood floor of the hall and the stairs on the way down to the front door. But what she saw at the bottom was nothing like what she expected.

The police were here.

Shifters and police did *not* mix. End of story. Shifters, according to the haters and even the general populace and definitely local law enforcement, were essentially criminals—or criminals-in-waiting. Their wolf nature was supposedly more prone to violence… all while it was *the humans* who went around blowing people up. And the police who looked the other way. What none of them would ever understand was that *the beast* was the best part of any shifter.

Terra planted her hands on her hips and ran a scrutinizing look over the hulking police officer who was occupying the doorway. He was tall and broad, muscular in a way that, for a human, meant he spent hours at the gym, worshiping his own body. Yet, she had to admit the effect was something worthy of worship. His trim black uniform fit just right over his bulging biceps, trim stomach, and muscular thighs. It was the kind of perfect male form that begged for her camera, and she couldn't help noticing with her artist's eye the details that would make him a heart-stopping subject—the deep sapphire blue of his eyes, the rough midnight black of his razor-short hair, the tension in his body that was a sort of relaxed power in the face of the gathering pack at the door. As gorgeous as his form may be, he was still a cop—which was to say, everything she loathed about humankind. This perfect male specimen wasn't something she was going to draw or photograph—this was the enemy come to her family's doorstep.

The coldness of his stare just drilled that fact home.

"What's this?" she asked, curling a lip of disgust at him.

"This is Officer Kaden Grant," Jaxson River said. He was the alpha of the River pack—he headed the Riverwise security company, and his family owned the safehouse. At one point, Terra thought he might be *the one* for her—a man strong enough to be her mate. He was an alpha's alpha, and when he had saved Cassie from the government thugs who had kidnapped her, Terra was certain Jaxson was the man who would finally break through her personal darkness.

But she'd been wrong.

Mating with Jaxson would've been the end—she would have been killed by the curse that haunted him. She had always known death was stalking her. She expected it to appear suddenly, like the car crash that had taken her mother. Like an unexpected magical curse in the man she thought would be her mate. Like Officer Kaden Grant, standing in her doorway and looking very much like the thing that would get her killed.

Jaxson was still talking. "Did Noah tell you about the video?" he asked her.

Noah nodded.

Terra said, "Sounds like my number is up."

"Terra… no." Jaxson stepped closer and put a hand on her shoulder. "We're not letting anything happen to you. Or anyone else. But in this latest video…"

Jaxson looked to Officer Grant, who had been coolly checking her out.

She narrowed her eyes. What the hell was that about?

WILD HEAT

Grant cleared his throat and snapped his eyes back up to hers. "The Wolf Hunter released another video just this morning, Ma'am." His voice was low and gruff. "The address of this house was listed as your current residence. However, in light of the recent WildLove bombings, the mayor has instructed the police department to take you into protective custody. He says you're *'An artist of renown, a jewel of our city.'*" Officer Grant gave the barest of smiles. "Which I guess means you rate a protective detail."

Terra drew back and gave Officer Grant another look of disgust. She turned to Jaxson. "Protective detail?"

"The safehouse is no longer safe. Especially for you." Jaxson's look was dead serious, and a new trickle of icy fear dripped slowly through Terra's chest and into her stomach, making it clench.

She turned back to Officer Grant. "Wait… the video said I was *here?* So you're saying the safehouse has been outed. Because of me."

"Not because of you," her cousin, Noah, insisted. "This maniac is calling you out, but he's really after everyone. I don't know how he found out about the safehouse—but there have been so many people going through this place in the last three months, it's a wonder it's been kept quiet this long."

11

Terra hadn't wanted to come to the safehouse in the first place—it was half prison and half refuge—but at least there were shifters here. *Her kind.* She and Cassie were safe here. And now the mayor wanted his police to watch over her—half of whom probably were secret hate group members.

It was a death sentence.

"We're *all* leaving the safehouse, Terra." Jaxson glowered at Officer Grant. "But there's nothing that says you have to go anywhere with this asshole. We'll find places for everyone, somehow, with friends, shifter families… we'll make it work."

Terra frowned. There were close to fifty people who have been living at the safehouse, since this madness started—Wilding pack, River pack, wolves that had been experimented on by the government, not to mention Mama River herself. "Really, Jaxson?" Terra asked. "How are you seriously going to find places for everyone?"

Jaxson's jaw worked, and she could tell he knew the size of the problem. Over two dozen shifters had been attracted to the news at the front door already, and there had to be a lightning-speed rumor running through the rest of the safehouse. Even Mama River, the matriarch of the River pack and keeper of the estate, was watching with careful eyes from the kitchen doorway.

"Ma'am." Officer Grant's deep voice pulled her back. "I promise you, we can offer a secure location for you—"

A commotion at the back of the crowd of shifters cut him off. It was her brother, Trent, pushing his way through the crowd.

"What the hell is going on here?" Trent shouted above the heads as he elbowed his way to the front. "Terra, what is this I hear about the police coming for you?" He glared at Officer Grant still lurking in the doorway but not coming inside.

"I'm not here to arrest her—" Officer Grant's voice ticked up a notch.

Terra ignored him and spoke directly to her brother. "There's a new video. The Wolf Hunter's after me now." Just saying the words out loud made her feel woozy again. She gripped the end of the stairwell banister. Jaxson's hand braced her, just as Noah's had before. She pushed him away, but then Trent shuffled forward to take his place.

"It's okay, Terra." Her brother was trying to calm her, but she was having none of it.

"It's *not* going to be okay!" she growled in his face. Her wolf was bristled out, ready to unsheathe claws on the next person who told her all of this was going to be *fine* when it was obvious that *nothing* was fine. And it never would be again.

Then she saw a small, dark-haired form pushing through the crowd, following in Trent's wake. *Cassie.* Her long, black hair danced around her thin shoulders, and her dark, dark eyes, just like their mother's, opened up into pools of fear and sadness when she arrived at Terra's side.

Oh God. She couldn't lose it in front of Cass. Couldn't give into the darkness, not now. Terra pushed Trent aside and went to her little sister. She kneeled down and wrapped her arms around her slender form. Her baby sister was only twelve and had barely started to live yet. She was about as big as a minute, and right now, she was shaking in Terra's arms. The girl had already been captured once, kidnapped right off the street outside her school, and whatever was after Terra—because this felt like the time when death would finally catch her—she needed to keep it the hell away from her little sister.

In that instant, she knew: *She would have to leave Cassie.* No matter how much that carved out her heart.

"You're going to be okay," Terra said, squeezing Cassie even tighter. "I promise, everything's going to be all right."

But her sister's eyes were still wide and freaked out when Terra pulled back. "Why is the Wolf Hunter after you?" she asked, her sweet voice tinged with fear.

Terra closed her eyes briefly, then opened them again. "I don't know, baby. There just are some evil people in this world." Her throat was closing up. She stood up, still holding Cassie's shoulders. "But the River pack is going to take care of you from now on."

Cassie's eyes went more round. "But I want to stay with *you.*"

God... a knife in her heart wouldn't hurt as much.

Jaxson took the cue and slid immediately to Cassie's side. "There's nothing to worry about, Cass. We'll find you a new home, even better than the safehouse."

Terra tried to show her gratitude in a look without words—because she was barely trusting herself to speak right now.

"Terra." Trent was shaking his head, and she knew what he was thinking: that they should stick together. But Jaxson's Riverwise security company had military experience, and Trent was a software developer. She sure as hell wasn't going to trust Cassie to her brother's care.

"You go wherever Jaxson tells you," she said

forcefully to Trent. If he fought her on this, she *would* bring the claws out. Then she softened her voice, for Cassie's sake. "Take her somewhere safe, Trent. Somewhere away from me. I'm the target now…" She had to clear her throat again. Every face was focused on her, so she spoke directly to them. "You *all* need to find safe places to go. *Now.*"

Trent pressed his lips together, but thankfully, he didn't argue.

"All right, everyone, listen up," Jaxson said, raising his voice and taking charge as he usually did. *Thank God.* "We need to relocate close to fifty shifters to safe locations, and we need to do it yesterday. This is not going to be a small operation. Everyone needs to stay calm and pitch in."

"I'm not going anywhere," Mama River spoke up from her spot in the doorway into the kitchen. "This is my home."

Terra couldn't help but smile, and it helped banish the tears that were threatening to fall. Mama River's defiance of her son, even though he was alpha of their pack, was just what she needed to hear. She'd grown to love Mama River more than she wanted to say out loud. Terra never had a mother, not since she was younger than Cassie, and

Mama River seemed to be a mother to anyone who walked through the door. If only her own father had been half the parent Mama River was, maybe Terra wouldn't have had to serve as Cassie's surrogate mother all the time they were growing up.

Not that she regretted a single moment of that.

Jaxson looked irritated, but not exactly surprised. "All right, everyone *except* my mother will need to find a new safe location. I'll take four volunteers who want to remain at the safehouse to guard Mama River and the estate in case Wolf Hunter decides to come after us."

Every hand in the room went up to volunteer. Terra wasn't surprised in the least.

"I said *four,*" Jaxson grumbled. "The rest of you are liabilities here, and I'm not taking any unnecessary risks." He looked down at Cassie, who had also raised her hand. "That includes you, short stuff. But before we move you out, how about you and Mama River help me pick who gets to stay?"

Cassie nodded at her new solemn duty and waded into the crowd, carefully checking out each face. A flush of pride and gratitude and a hundred other emotions ran through Terra, threatening to pull her apart at the seams. Jaxson was mated and would never be hers—but he was the kind of alpha who could have been right for her if the fates hadn't been working against them. Or really, just against *her.*

She had no illusions about which one of them death was stalking.

On impulse, Terra threw her arms around Jaxson, hugged him briefly, and let him go. "Thank you," she said, quietly, then she turned to the hulking police officer at her door.

His expression was inscrutable, but there was something lurking behind those dark blue eyes—a smoldering something that made her wolf sit up and take notice. Of course, there were alphas in the human world—Terra knew that, even if she didn't consort with humans except from behind her lens. That didn't mean her wolf should be responding to one.

Had to be all the emotions tumbling through her and crossing her wires.

She strode up to Officer Grant and glared up at his stone-chiseled face. "I'll go with you now."

Trent appeared at her side. "Terra, what the hell? You can't trust the police."

Jaxson was also back to scowling at Officer Grant. "Look, we've got a bomber from the WildLove case still in our custody. How about you take him instead?"

"I can send a squad car up to pick him up," Officer Grant said coolly. "But I've been assigned to Ms. Wilding's case."

Jaxson turned back to her. "We'll find another place for you, Terra. You don't have to go with this guy. I don't care what the mayor says."

"If the police take me into protective custody," she said, keeping her voice calm, "then the Wolf Hunter will be looking for me there. And *I'm* the one he's after. I'm sure the police will keep me safe. Let the Wolf Hunter spin his wheels trying to find me while you get everyone else hidden away."

Trent gritted his teeth. "That makes no sense at all."

She gave him a steely look. "I need my equipment, Trent. Just the cameras. They're in my room."

Her brother's eyes flashed, but it was all anger and no fight—he wouldn't try to stop her now, but he'd give her hell about it later. Jaxson was scowling at her too. Only Officer Grant was giving her a slightly approving tilt of his head, but that could've just been her imagination.

She gestured angrily to the officer to move his giant bulk out of the doorway, then strode past him out into the early afternoon sunshine. His black-and-white police car was parked just outside.

This was it. This was how it was going to end. Her mother's death was tragic and senseless—a car crash on the interstate. At least Terra's would have some purpose. She would buy Cassie a little time to get away. Far from her. *Safe.*

And Terra would live every moment she had left with no regrets.

CHAPTER 2

K aden watched as Terra hauled in her cameras—all three gigantic black bags worth.

After a tense and silent drive down the mountains to the far side of Seattle, they had finally reached the police department's safehouse. It wasn't much more than a dingy cinderblock cube, but it was in a relatively benign neighborhood and pretty well isolated, far from anyone's gang territory. Most of all, the department had maintained occupancy continuously for years with one criminal or another—someone turning states' evidence or part of a witness relocation program—all without discovery or incident. It was the perfect place to stash someone for a while. Only Terra Wilding was no ordinary criminal or witness.

"Let me help you with that," Kaden said, reaching for her bags before she got too far.

Terra gave him a look so dark, he thought she might actually go for his throat if he touched the bags. Then she turned her back on him and marched up to the door.

It had been this way during the entire drive—angry looks, barely repressed growls that he could still hear, and enough agitation in that skinny little body of hers to light up half the city. She was treating him just like every shifter treated a human, namely like dirt. What was he thinking, taking on this assignment?

Oh, right—that he didn't want his department fucking it up.

Shifters were no good punks… for the most part. Kaden had seen more fucked up shifter rituals when he was growing up than he cared to remember, but his childhood was nothing like the flat-out brutality he saw as a cop on patrol in shifter gang territory. If this Wolf Hunter person had targeted the gangs, Kaden would've thrown him a party, along with the rest of his department.

But this girl was different.

She was a poor little rich kid with no mother who turned into celebrated artist... and dammit, those were the kind of people the Seattle Police Department was supposed to protect.

Not to mention, she was hot as hell, with her dark shirt clinging to her chest, skinny leggings emphasizing her mile-long legs, and silvery jewelry banging around on her wrists. That raven-black hair went everywhere, and even though her dark-charcoaled eyes glared at him most of the time, there was no question a lot was going on behind them.

Plus she had a rear end he couldn't stop staring at.

He had forgotten how hot shifter women could be... and how they could stir up his blood. Especially the feisty ones.

He punched in the code for the electronic lock and barely swung open the front door before she barged ahead of him. Kaden sucked in a breath, counted to three in his head, and let it out slow as he followed after. No matter how she treated him, he was going to do his damn job and keep her safe anyway.

Once they were inside the apartment, she prowled around like she was sniffing out the place. There wasn't much to see. The house was small and sparsely furnished—just a tiny couch, an old TV, and a glass dining set that could barely hold breakfast for two. But it had a full kitchen, two bedrooms, and a bath—enough for one or more people in protective custody to stay with their handlers. That's what he really was—or at least what he signed up for. His extensive work with the shifter gangs in the city had earned him the opportunity to be the liaison in this case. That, and he argued for it, knowing the three other most-likely candidates for the job would completely fuck it up.

And probably get this girl killed.

"There are two bedrooms in the back," Kaden called as Terra headed that direction, stomping her big black boots across the worn, beige carpet. "Pick whichever one you like."

She disappeared around the corner, and sounds of revulsion came flooding back out of the hall. Several soft curses as well.

Kaden stood awkwardly in the middle of the small livingroom, wondering where to even start with her. She seemed righteously pissed off, and he couldn't decide if it was because of *him* or the Wolf Hunter or just the sad state of the apartment. Maybe all three. Kaden had done his research, so he knew a few things about her. Terra Wilding, the up-and-coming artist, was the daughter of Donnie Wilding, local entrepreneur who hit it big in some dot-com-type business. Upshot was that the family was rolling in money. Which made Terra something of a Seattle Princess. Hauling her out of that luxury estate in the mountains and down to the dregs where normal people lived had to be a shock to her system.

He smirked as she banged around in the bedroom, but it quickly died. Truth was, knowing she had money didn't tell him anything about the girl behind those dark eyes. There was a lot going on under the hood with her, he could tell.

And those eyes were already pulling him in.

Which was not smart. Getting involved was *not* on the agenda, and not just because it was crossing all kinds of ethical boundaries.

She was a *wolf.* And that was flat dangerous to him.

He cleared his throat. "You'll be safe as long as you're here," he called out from the spot where he'd planted himself. He might as well lay out the rules while she was still riding that first wave of shock. "But we have to keep your presence here on the down low. That means no phone calls, no email that's not authorized, no leaving the apartment without me. We'll have meals brought in, and you might be allowed to leave once a week or so if we can get authorization and backup for an outing."

She tromped back out of the bedroom hallway, but she still had those three bulky black camera bags slung over her shoulders.

She brushed past him, heading for the front door. "I'm not staying here."

What? Kaden dashed after her, just barely catching her before she flung it open. "Excuse me?"

She whirled on him and stared fiercely up at him. She wasn't exactly short—in fact, she was relatively tall and slender, but still stacked with those shifter muscles and curvy in all the right places, the way shifter women were. But Kaden was taller than most men, let alone women.

He towered over her.

"You can't hold me here against my will!" she spat.

He held up his hands. "I thought you signed up for this. Did I miss something?"

She just glared at him. "I left the Riverwise safehouse so my family would go into hiding without me. *I'm* the one who's endangering everyone now. *I'm* the one the

Wolf Hunter is after. They needed to get away from me, and you were a convenient way to get away from them."

What was she talking about? He frowned. "You realize you're actually in danger here."

She snorted with disgust, and it would've been cute except she was giving him a look that seemed designed to cut him down the size. "As if you're going to protect me."

That brought the heat up to his face. "Yes, actually, that's the idea."

"You want to protect me?" she threw in his face. "Go catch the Wolf Hunter!"

That raised the hairs on the back of his neck. "The department is doing everything it can to track down that lunatic."

"Really?" she asked, leaning back and crossing her arms. She looked like she was trying to figure out if he was just stupid or if he was actually lying to her. "Because they haven't done jack until now. Don't pretend you care about shifters. You don't. You're only doing this because your boss has ordered you to. Because the mayor will look bad if someone in *Artist Today* is killed in his city. He doesn't give a damn that this hate group and their leader have been hunting my family all this time. They're blowing them up, for God's sake!"

Kaden kept his mouth shut, but her words were making him squirm. Because he knew all that was likely true. Which was why he wanted to be her handler in the first place.

"Well, I take my job seriously. And I have every intention of keeping you safe."

She shook her head like he was pathetic. "Look, I get it. You're just a guy, doing his job. This isn't your fault. But I'm not going to sit around and put up with this charade. I've already lost one uncle. I've got a baby sister who was kidnapped once already. I'm not taking any chances with her or with any of my family again. So if the Wolf Hunter wants me—let him come and get me!"

She put her hand on the doorknob like she was ready to flee outside.

This girl has some kind of a death wish. Kaden locked his hand around her wrist and yanked her hand off the doorknob.

Terra growled and turned on him—suddenly her claws were out and heading for his face. He grabbed hold of her other wrist and held both of her hands away from his face… and anything else they might shred with their razor sharpness. Then he slowly backed her against the wall and pinned her hands there. She was struggling against him, wide-eyed at his strength, but it was quickly becoming clear that, even with her shifter muscles, she was no match for him.

"Rule number one while you're here," he said calmly, still pinning her to the wall, "don't even think about threatening me with those things." He glanced at her claws.

Frustration and surprise scrunched up her face. She tried again to get free and couldn't. Then a dawning realization changed her expression to a frown—shifter women were freaking *strong,* and they knew it. He was big, but a mere human shouldn't be able to hold her this way.

He released her and stepped back quickly before she could think that through.

She slowly lowered her hands, but she was eyeing him with suspicion.

Dammit, he might've blown this already.

"I could have shifted out of your hold," she said, watching him carefully.

"You could've shredded my face," he retorted. "And I don't get paid enough for disfigurement. Besides, the department health plan just isn't that great."

She glanced at the door and then back at him. "You

can't keep me here."

She was back on point with wanting to leave. He kept the sigh of relief inside, where she wouldn't see. "No, I can't. But you're a fool if you walk out that door. I'm the best chance you have of staying alive."

She narrowed her eyes, studying him. She took a long time about it, too, starting at his boots and sliding her hot gaze all the way up. He worked damn hard to keep his physical reaction off his face, but *man,* it was stirring him around to have her examine him that way. He ticked through all his training and experience in dealing with unstable, angry shifters on the streets. Somehow it was easier to keep calm with those punks than with this skinny, little girl. *Woman,* he corrected himself. She was definitely 100% grown-up female shifter, even if she was only twenty-one. And she was getting under his skin way too easily. If he really wanted to protect her, he couldn't let that happen.

When her gaze finally returned to his face, her expression was softer, open. Her eyes had gone round, and the deep liquid centers were dilated. *Good God,* she was pretty, and with her looking at him in that soulful way… he could see it now. Why she was the darling of the mayor and whatever high-brow society she hung out with.

He waited for her to say something, determined to be cool and follow her lead. Because she was right—she could walk out that door, and there was no way he could really keep her. And her chances truly were better with him at the safehouse than anywhere else in the city.

She pursed her lips for a second, then said, "I need my equipment. My darkroom supplies. I can set up in the smaller room."

Relief trickled through him. "I'll work on getting your equipment moved. And I'll do whatever I can to make sure you're comfortable. I expect you'll be here for a while."

"I doubt that," she said softly. Her gaze had dropped to his chest, but she wasn't really looking at him. Her eyes had gone dull, lost their sheen, and the sudden vulnerability of her far-away look made him want to reach out and pull her into a hug.

Which was *not* going to happen.

Get a grip, Kaden. "There shouldn't be a problem with modifying your room to suit your needs. I'll get started on it right away." He held a hand out to take one of her camera bags. "In the meantime, why don't you let me help you with that?"

He waited with his hand outstretched, letting her bridge the gap and close the distance.

She blinked at the floor for good five seconds, saying nothing.

He waited. Patient. There was some kind of war going on inside her that he didn't really understand, but he wanted to. Which was another dangerous thing for him.

Eventually, she unhooked one of the straps from her shoulder and dropped the camera bag into his outstretched hand. Then she turned without a word and headed toward the back bedroom again. He watched her disappear around the corner and decided to give her a moment before following.

Besides, he needed to get his own head together.

He angled for this assignment because he wanted to make sure the girl actually stayed alive. And now that he had met her, he could see why the mayor, even though he was human, wanted her under protective custody. The city losing someone like her wasn't acceptable. Kaden didn't know anything about art, but he could already see something special in the artist. And just looking at some of her work during his research, he saw something he'd always been looking for in the city, but never really found—the good parts. The parts he wanted to believe were there. That he wanted to protect.

But if Terra Wilding figured out who he was, all of that would go to hell.

Including his ability to keep her safe.

CHAPTER 3

L ess than twenty-four hours later, Terra was going out of her mind.

She paced her tiny bedroom, but it didn't help. She'd transformed the space into a darkroom, rearranged the sparse furniture in the house three times, and managed to avoid seven conversations with her very hot bodyguard/jailer Officer Kaden Grant. He seemed to think his job required making small talk, but that was the very last thing she could stand at the moment. And every time she caught him looking at her with those blazing blue eyes, her wolf started to pant... which was just insane!

He was human.

She'd never been with a human before, and now was not the time to start... no matter how much her body was itching for a distraction and her wolf was hungering for *him*. Which made no sense at all—most male wolves weren't alpha enough to hold her attention; how could a human get her wolf all tied up in knots? The answer was simple, even if Terra didn't want to face it: she was emotionally wrung out, and the stress of waiting for a madman to find her and kill her was playing games with her head and her wolf.

She was in a fragile state. She had to be careful.

Which was why she'd spent the last day hiding out in her bedroom and staying far from the hot temptation in the livingroom. That was the best way to avoid something she would regret. But it was a sign of the depth of her mania that she couldn't stop thinking about the way Officer Grant filled out his clothes. He'd traded his squad car and uniform for a nondescript tan sedan and simple jeans and t-shirt—but those worn-looking jeans were perfectly snug around his muscular thighs, and that t-shirt clung to his chest like he owed it a favor.

In a word, he was freaking *hot…* and her body was constantly betraying her in wanting all those muscles pressed up, hard, against her.

The whole thing was driving her mad.

When her laptop pinged an incoming Skype call, she nearly cried out with happiness. Officer Grant had gotten clearance for her to take certain calls, but nothing had come through right away. She hustled over to the bed, cradling the machine and tapping to accept the call. It was from Cassie, and her bright, shining smile lit up the screen. Terra couldn't help smiling in return. Sometimes Cassie was the only thing that reminded her what life and living were really about.

"You're not going to believe this!" Cassie gushed.

"Believe what?" Terra laced her fingers and propped her chin on them, leaning forward so Cassie would know she had all of Terra's attention.

"We're staying with a real family!" Cassie said. "They're shifters, but they haven't been outed. They have two boys and one girl and two cats, one of which is really black and has tons of fur and extra toes!"

Terra felt a weird urge to giggle rising up through her, but it didn't quite reach the surface. "Extra toes? Sounds like trouble to me."

Cassie nodded solemnly. "Oh yeah. Definitely trouble. She's always chasing after the other one. I scolded her and told her I have bigger claws than she does, so she better behave."

This time, Terra couldn't hold back the laugh, but it dissolved into a kind of sickly snort, and she shut it down fast. Didn't want Cassie to know how close to the edge she was... more than normal. "That's awesome, Cass. So this family... are they nice?"

"Oh man, I didn't think anybody could be as nice as Mama River," Cassie said. "But this lady—her name is Lillian—is *so* nice. She makes us special snacks for our lunches and treats me like I'm one of her kids. I mean, not really—I know I'm not—but I can tell. She's trying really hard to make me feel like I'm part of the family."

Terra had to blink back the tears. It was a valiant effort and ultimately successful. "That's fantastic, Cassie." She couldn't say any more. Terra remembered their mom, even if Cassie didn't—she was warm and funny, but a terribly bad cook. All the time Cassie was growing up, Terra tried to be *her*—funny and kind, and even burning dinner every once in a while just to re-create what they'd lost. Their father had disappeared into his

ALISA WOODS

work, and it was up to her and Trent to be the mom and dad... only they were just kids themselves.

And now Cassie had a new mom.

"I really like it here," her baby sister said, "but I miss you."

That was all Terra could take. She pressed her palm to the screen, and Cassie followed by pressing hers against it as well. They were touching nothing but glass, but Terra's heart swelled so much it ached. Tears leaked from the sides of her eyes.

"Are you doing your lessons?" Terra sniffed and tried to wipe her eyes without being obvious.

"I didn't even tell you—that's the best part! I get to go to school again!"

Terror rushed through Terra. *"What?* When did this happen? You've only been there for a day."

"I know, but Lillian says—"

"Does Trent know about this?" Terra interrupted her. When Cassie was snatched by the government thugs who were doing experiments on shifters, they'd taken her right off the street outside her old private school. The one her father had absently picked without checking to see if it was a decent place. A *secure* place.

Cassie's smile faded. "Trent says it's okay if *you* say it's

38

okay." Her sister's big, round eyes, filling up with the sadness of the world, just about killed her. *"Please,* Terra. I've been at the safehouse *forever.* I just want to meet some new friends."

Guilt tore at her. Terra wasn't a people-person *at all*— she was at home behind the lens, where that distancing shot allowed her to keep the cold realities of the world at lens-length—but Cassie was a budding extrovert. She was whimsical, social, and just a general spreader of joy. If Terra was going crazy being cooped up, Cassie had to be going out of her mind completely.

But Terra couldn't lose her. Not again.

"Let me talk to Trent, honey," she said softly. "I'm sure we can work out something to make sure you're safe."

Cassie brightened immediately. "Okay." She left the screen but was back an instant later. "Oh, and by the way, my name is no longer Cassie." She said this very solemnly. "My name is now Shelley." She leaned into the camera and whispered, "It's part of my secret identity. We're undercover, you know."

That forced a smile on Terra's face again. "Okay, *Shelley…* go get Trent for me, okay?"

Cassie nodded and disappeared from the screen. Terra

heard her tromp through her new idyllic home, calling for their brother. Terra let her shoulders drop, already exhausted by the kaleidoscope of emotions.

A moment later, Trent appeared on the screen. He scanned her face, glanced over his shoulder, apparently checking for Cassie, then turned back to her. "You look like hell," he said with a frown.

Terra smacked the screen and sent it backward on the bed. It was now face up, its keyboard dangling in the air, and Trent was getting a good shot of the ceiling.

His voice squawked in protest. "Okay, okay! I'm sorry! I was just concerned about you." Trent paused. "Jesus, Terra, give me a break, will you?"

She righted the laptop and scowled at him. "What is this about sending Cassie to school?"

His hunched-up shoulders dropped. "So that's what you're pissed about. It's really hard to tell with you sometimes, sis."

No, but it will do as a substitute. "I told you to keep her *safe*. Why are you promising to let her roam out in public with all these maniacs out there?"

"Come on!" Anger flashed in his eyes. "Give me some credit. I'm not going to put Cass in danger. But I can't homeschool her the way you were doing at the safehouse.

And Lillian's doing enough, taking her in."

The tears were threatening to surface again. "I can't lose her again, Trent."

His expression softened. "I know. Don't worry. I've got it handled."

"How?" She knew in her heart that Trent wasn't like their father—he wouldn't abandon Cassie right when she needed him most—but she still needed to hear the details. And her twin brother, younger by about two minutes, knew her well enough not to fight her on that.

"It's a small, private school," he explained. "Tuition is insane, so it's very exclusive. I made a donation in Dad's name, so they're being very accommodating with the new identity thing. Plus one of the Riverwise security guys will be escorting her there and back, every day."

Terra pursed her lips and searched for some hole in her brother's plan, but there was nothing she could argue against.

Trent paused for a moment. "All we need is your go-ahead. Cassie won't go if you don't approve of it."

That pushed her over the edge. "Okay." She sighed. "I know she's feeling crazed with all this hiding out. I'm going out of my mind, too. I need to get out. Go on a shoot or something. I need new material."

Trent's eyes narrowed. "I thought you were locked down at this police safehouse."

"I am." She huffed her frustration and swept her hair back from her face.

"What are they actually doing to keep you safe?" The anger was back on his face. "You know I don't trust those guys."

"I'm *fine.*" She waved him off. The last thing she needed was for Trent to get wound up about her again... and start demanding she join Cassie in her new perfect-family hideout. "And it's just the one guy watching over me—Officer Grant—and he's harmless." Well, not exactly *harmless...* but she was convinced he wasn't a shifter-hater. With the looks he was giving her, he might be one of those humans who was secretly fascinated by shifters and wanted to bed down with one. Usually, male wolves hooked up with female humans—the WildLove app was all about scratching that itch—but it could certainly go the other way. There just weren't that many female wolves around... but there were undoubtedly human men curious for a taste of wolf.

Her inner wolf was panting hard at that idea.

God, it was like her hormones were on overdrive. *What the hell?* She really needed to *get out.* And away from

Officer McHottie.

"I know that look," Trent said, obviously not too happy about it, either. "You're planning something."

"I just need to *do* something," she said, growling out her frustration. "Before I go out of my mind."

"Jesus, Terra." The concern ramped up on his face. "Don't do anything stupid. *Please.*"

"Thanks for the confidence." She turned the growl in his direction.

"I mean it," he said, his anger returning. "You need to stay put until this is all sorted out. For Cassie's sake. Think about what it would do to her if you got yourself killed." The strain in his voice just reminded her that her brother actually did care about her. And he was probably right.

She still gave him a glare. "I promise not to be stupid."

He nodded, but still looked uncertain.

"Gotta go," she said and closed the laptop before Trent could say anything more. With a growl, she shoved it away from her, and it slid nearly to the edge of the bed, but stopped. She started to pace her room again, but that was just making her *more* crazy. Instead, she hunted around for her boots—they were stuffed under the bed—pulled them on, and stomped out of her room.

She caught Officer Grant by surprise—he was hovering over his phone, sitting on the dingy couch—and he practically leaped to his feet, instantly alert as she barreled out of her room. She didn't even know what she was planning, she just needed some air. She ignored his inquiring look, strode over to the window, and threw back the curtains. The afternoon sunshine leaked through the blinds, but she still couldn't see anything, much less open the window. The cords were a tangled mess, and she yanked them to no effect—then she growled and yanked harder.

"Is there a problem?" Officer Grant asked from behind her. He'd crept up on her from the couch, and his masculine scent washed over her—earthy and sharp, like a hike on a winter's day. Her wolf whined for her to turn around and take a bite.

Jesus. Coming out of her room was probably a mistake.

Terra nearly yanked the blinds right off the wall. Then she curled up her fists and stared at the still-closed white slats. *"No."*

"That *no* sounds an awful lot like *yes.*" Officer Grant had moved even closer.

She gestured to the blinds. "Do you have any idea

how symbolic this is?"

"Um... no?" He was right behind her now.

"My world has telescoped down to *this*." She flicked her fingers at the blinds. "Voluntary jail bars, holding me in and blinding me by cutting off the real world. It's an impenetrable blank slate, barren of *life*."

"You're trapped in a box." The calmness of his voice and his words flushed something through her—heat, attraction, relief that he *understood*. She kept all of this locked inside, not wanting to let him know how much that affected her.

"This is a killing box. I need to get *out*. I need to... *I need my art*." The last words came out in a whisper. She knew how weak it sounded, but she couldn't help it. She turned around to face him. "I don't expect you to understand."

His face was inscrutable again, closed off and shut down. "You don't expect much of me, do you?"

Her mouth hung open for a second. *He was right*. She was treating him horribly, especially given he obviously *did* understand, at least somewhat.

She dropped her gaze to the floor, cheeks hot. "I'm sorry," she mumbled. "None of this is your fault."

He was peering at her, trying to catch her gaze, but

she couldn't let him... that fragile feeling was back, like the pieces of her might blow apart with the slightest breeze. Or a heated look from him. She crossed her arms over her chest and stared doggedly off to the side at the blank wall of the livingroom.

He sighed, but when he spoke, his voice was soft. "It's completely normal to go stir crazy after a while. I was hoping for more than a day—"

She whipped her gaze to meet his. *"A day?* I've been hiding out for months. *Months.* The box is different—smaller, tighter around my neck—but the prison is the same."

The kindness in his eyes made her look away again.

"It's going to be rough, but you'll get through this, Terra," he said. "It's my job to make sure you do, and I've got a damn near perfect record in the department. I'm not screwing that up." He was joking with her, but the humor didn't reach her. Couldn't unspool the tension that was tying her in knots.

"Can we at least open the blinds?" she asked, not looking at him.

"Sorry, no. Not safe." But his voice was gentle.

"Can I look out?" Still not looking.

"Can't risk anyone seeing you."

"I'll get my camera."

"Terra—"

She turned to him, pleading for his understanding with her eyes. "I have to do *something.*"

He hesitated, and in that moment, a hundred different emotions seemed to flit across his face, so fast Terra wasn't even sure what they were. But in that moment, all she wanted was her camera in her hand, and this handsome emotive human man in her lens frame...

His face settled into something inscrutable again. "Okay. The camera. But nothing more."

That enlivened her, and she dashed around him to nearly sprint back to her room. Maybe she would poke the lens through the blinds and hope for something other than an alley outside. Or maybe, she would turn her lens on the most alive thing in this small, dingy hideout... Officer Kaden Grant.

She dug through her bag and was halfway back to the livingroom, when her phone buzzed in her back pocket. She dug it out and glanced at the face. It was a message from her friend, Sally. Dark haired, older but still beautiful, with a taste for Terra's art.

Officer Grant was striding quickly to her side. "What is it?"

She showed it to him, but the alert quickly faded. "A message from a gallery owner in downtown Seattle."

Officer Grant frowned.

Terra swiped it open and quickly read. "She has a private collector who wants to meet with me. Something about being interested in my art." She looked up. "She says it's a friend of the mayor."

Officer Grant's frown just deepened. "I don't like it."

"But this is great! Just what I need to keep from—"

He held up a finger to stop her while pulling out his own phone. "Don't reply. Don't do anything. Let me check this out."

She bit her lip while he made a call, excitement and tension taking turns pummeling her stomach. He was talking quickly with someone on the other line. The frown just grew deeper, and when he got off the phone, he hesitated before turning to her.

"Apparently, this is legit. The mayor himself has approved this contact. Says something about it being good for the city." He frowned. "I still don't like it."

"Yes!" She threw her arms up in the air in victory.

That drew a small smile onto Officer Grant's face. "All right, all right. Pack your cameras or whatever. I'll set up the meet. Make sure we're not taking any stupid chances. I don't care if it's the mayor's illegitimate child holding him ransom, I'm not risking your safety in any way with this."

His protectiveness flushed even more happiness through her, chasing after the glee that was already running circles through her body.

"I'll get my stuff together." She skipped off to the bedroom.

It wasn't until he was out of sight that Terra realized this was the first time she'd seen Officer Grant smile.

CHAPTER 4

K aden didn't like this at all.

He and Terra were in the car heading to downtown. Apparently this meetup had been approved all the way up the chain of command to the mayor, so it wasn't like Kaden had an option to say no. But every fiber of his being was screaming *no fucking way!* There was something seriously off about taking someone who was in protective custody *out* of protective custody and driving them to the middle of downtown to meet a complete stranger—even if that stranger was some kind of personal friend of the mayor. Kaden was savvy enough to know how things worked, especially in the SPD—the mayor's "personal friend" was probably a political donor. Or someone he owed a favor. Or someone's cousin's brother's next-door-neighbor who had something on the mayor himself. It was political bullshit. And there were way too many ways that could get Terra killed. He just couldn't control everything once they stepped outside the safehouse door.

But this decision wasn't up to him.

Terra beamed in the passenger seat next to him. He couldn't deny the change in her now that she was outside and working. She'd had her camera glued to her face almost the entire drive, snapping up shots of... something. He wasn't quite sure what, but she had changed lenses a couple of times and swapped out the memory card at least twice. He had to admit he liked the smile on her face.

If only this weren't so stupid-dangerous.

She seemed totally unconcerned... at least at the moment. The girl was maddening. Angry as fuck one minute, despondent with those big black eyes the next. It didn't really matter what end of the emotional spectrum she was on—all of it triggered a huge need in him to protect her. It was his job, of course, but it was more than that. Somehow she had sunk under his skin, and protecting her had become *personal*. Not the kind of personal where he was tearing off her clothes and exploring her body with his—he kept having to remind himself that *wasn't* on the menu—but when she had that lost look in her eyes, all he wanted to do was kiss it away.

He pulled the sedan into an underground parking garage. Terra put her camera away, tucking it into the black bag resting on the seat. Her smile dimmed as they slid into the darkness. Kaden circled around until he could find a spot that was close to both the elevator and the public exit. He wanted to have a lot of options for an easy retreat back to the car.

He put it in park and turned to her. "All right, let's get this straight. We're going in, we're talking to this art collector person, and then we're leaving. No dawdling. No hanging out any longer than we need to."

"Understood." Although the readiness with which she agreed unsettled him. He expected more push back.

"I mean it, Terra." He had to hold in his frustration. "My job here is to keep you safe. To do that, you have to do what I say."

She lifted her camera and pointed it at him, snapping a few shots of his mouth wide open because he couldn't figure out what the hell she was doing. The impish grin on her face was almost worth the shock punching holes through his brain. Then she tucked the camera away and smiled in a way that blasted the thoughts straight out of his head.

Jesus, he was in trouble with this girl.

"In and out," she said around her smile. "That's all. Promise."

He sighed and gave her a short nod. They climbed out of the car, and before they even hit the street, she had her camera out again.

This section of downtown was pretty upscale—glitzy stores selling overpriced handbags, jewelry showcases fit for the Princess of Monaco, and several cafés with the kind of healthy food that Seattle hipsters liked to eat. The art gallery was tucked between a coffeehouse and a bookstore, only a block down from the parking garage.

Terra stowed her camera, seeming to find less of interest on the streets now. Or maybe she was just getting ready to meet the gallery owner.

Kaden held the door for her. The wide glass storefront let in all kinds of natural light, and the paintings and photographs on display were printed on oversized canvases and mounted on partitions scattered haphazardly around the open floor of the gallery. It was like a maze that forced you to wind past all the different types of art, each with their own explanatory note card. Kaden knew absolutely nothing about painting or photography, and frankly, he had no opinion about any of the actual works, but the gallery itself was a security nightmare. There could be a hundred hate-group bombers hiding behind the partitions, and he would never see them until it was too late.

He stuck close to Terra's side, his hand hovering near the small of her back but not touching. His hand itched to bridge that final three inches, but she didn't seem to even notice his nearness. She just strode across the gallery floor, sporting a wide smile for the older woman in back who was hurrying toward them. The gallery owner was dressed all in black, covering every square inch of her stick-thin body, all the way up to the shockingly purple scarf wound around her neck. Her giant, double-hoop earrings tinkled as she embraced Terra.

The hug went on forever. "Oh my God, Terra, I've been so worried and horrified by all these events." The woman's face was devoid of makeup, and her horrified expression was made more severe by the tightly-pulled-back bun in her hair and her squeezed-shut eyes. "These videos are an abomination! And now…" She pulled back and held Terra's cheeks in her hands. "And now, my child, they are after *you!* How can you even endure it?"

Kaden had to hold in his growl. This woman was seriously *not helping* with the over-the-top drama about the threats to Terra. The videos themselves were bad enough.

Terra hugged the woman again, squeezing her hard. "It's okay, Sally, I promise. I'm fine." She drew back and gestured to Kaden behind her. "See? I've got my own personal bodyguard."

Sally eyed him, head to toe. "Yes, you do." It was more than a little creepy, being checked out by a woman three times his age. She was older than his mother, and his mother may have been many things, but she didn't chase after younger guys. Although, truth be told, he hadn't talked to his mother in so long, he honestly didn't know what she did anymore. He left that life behind when he refused to get swept up in the gangs.

"This is Officer Kaden Grant," Terra said. "He's taking good care of me."

"Well, I'm so pleased to hear that." Sally stepped forward and extended her hand. "Terra is a jewel, a rare talent, and you absolutely *must* do everything you can to protect her." The creepiness of before was lessened by her obviously genuine concern for Terra.

At least they shared that. "The best way I can protect her is to minimize the amount of time we're here today." Kaden tipped his head to Sally. "No offense, Ma'am."

"None taken." But she dropped his hand and stepped back. "But of course we should transact our business quickly." She turned to Terra. "Your new patron is awaiting you in the back. Follow me." Then she whisked away, her ballet-slippered feet silent on the concrete flooring. She quickly disappeared around a partition, heading through the maze toward the back.

Kaden stuck close to Terra again as they followed after.

Terra tipped her head back and whispered, "Please excuse Sally—I think she hits on every man who walks through the door."

That forced a grin on his face. "Is that what she was doing?"

"Oh, come on! Don't tell me you didn't notice her checking you out." Terry gave him a small scowl that had his body reacting far too much.

"I have no idea what you're talking about."

Terra rolled her eyes, but they had to stop speaking because they had reached the back. Sally ushered them through a white door that blended seamlessly into the wall. On the other side was the storage part of the gallery with wrapped paintings and stacked boxes lining the walls of a cavernous warehouse. A man stood a dozen feet away in a trim, tailored suit—Kaden immediately pegged him for some kind of money. Mid-30s, well-muscled but lean, piercing blue eyes and dark hair—and the kind that seemed used to getting the things he wanted.

Kaden instantly disliked him.

Sally introduced him. "Terra, this is Julius McGovern. He comes highly recommended by the mayor. It seems they share quite an appreciation for your work."

Julius smiled, and his eyes raked over Terra in a way that set Kaden's teeth on edge. Then the man crossed the concrete floor and swept Terra's hands into his own. His gaze roamed her face like it was a piece of art he was inspecting, then he leaned in and kissed her quickly, once on each cheek.

Kaden had to stop his immediate impulse, which was to throw the guy across the room. His violent need to keep this asshole from touching Terra was so strong it shocked him—and that surprise held him in place more than anything else.

Terra seemed startled as well. Just as Kaden was about to shut that shit down, Julius spoke up. "Please forgive me, my dear Terra." His smile was oily and pretentious. "I'm a little awestruck by your beauty, and your art has already entered my heart and rendered me senseless."

Terra seemed to relax, but that bullshit just set Kaden even more on edge. Was this how they talked in the art world, for fuck's sake? It sounded borderline stalker to him, but what did he know about art collectors? Maybe he was just a normal fan. Kaden took his cue from Terra, who seemed to glow under the man's praise.

"I don't quite know what to say to that," she stumbled. And Kaden had to admit the blush on her pale cheeks was more than a little attractive.

Julius seemed to notice too, and Kaden practically growled out loud when the man lifted his hand to her cheek to lightly stroke the blush there. "What a treasure you are," he said softly. Thankfully, he backed off after that, dropping Terra's hands and opening a little space between them.

Kaden's rage response ratcheted down a notch. *Fuck.* Either he was reading this all wrong or his hair-trigger protective instinct with Terra had a reason for wanting to rip the guy's head off. Either way, he was glad Julius was backing the hell off.

"Obviously, I'm a tremendous fan of your work." He flicked a look to Kaden but seemed to dismiss his presence as irrelevant and turned back to Terra. "And I have a proposal for you, my dear, if you'd be so kind as to hear me out. "

"Of course." Excitement filled Terra's voice. "I'm already grateful just to have this excuse to get out and discuss art again. You have no idea how much of a relief it is."

Julius clapped his hands together with delight. "Even better!" He leaned forward and dropped his voice. "I've been thinking that this whole nonsense with the videos and the Wolf Hunter must be setting you terribly on edge. And I thought to myself, Julius, what can you do to help this poor young woman in this terrible situation? And the answer came to me in a flash of insight." He snapped his fingers in the air. "I hope you'll indulge me for a moment while I explain."

Terra nodded eagerly. "I'm very intrigued."

Julius gestured vaguely to the wrapped-up artwork around them. "Your previous work is astonishing and brilliant—you shine a light on the darker side of Seattle and bring out this tremendous vibrancy. Even those of us who know and love the city already have had our understanding deepened by it, but for those outside of Seattle, you've created an image for the city, a beating heart of humanity, that it didn't have before. It's a sign of the depth of your talent that you've been able to capture the imagination of so many. But now, with this new revelation of the shifters among us… and all the rampant hate and prejudice that has flooded into the public sphere… I can't help thinking that you, *especially* as a shifter artist, are uniquely positioned to explore that new aspect of our community."

Terra's dark eyes lit up. "How do you mean?"

Julius beckoned her with a single crooked finger, and she eased closer. Kaden's alarm levels went up again when the man dropped a hand on her shoulder.

"I would like to commission some work from you," he said.

Kaden had to hold in his growl. "What sort of work?"

All three of them—Sally, the gallery owner, Julius, the sleazy art patron, and Terra—whipped startled looks to him, as if he wasn't expected to speak during this entire enterprise. *Of course.* He was just the hired muscle. But dammit, he was here to make sure she stayed safe, and

Julius seemed like trouble waiting to happen. It wasn't simply because every time Julius touched her, Kaden wanted to flatten his pretentious face.

"Well…" Julius arched an eyebrow at Kaden, but then quickly directed his gaze back to Terra. "I would like you to create a series of works. It would be something like "The People of Seattle." Only instead of photographing humans, in these works, you'll be examining *shifters*—but not in their human forms."

Terra frowned. "You mean photographing shifters as wolves?"

"Exactly!" Julius shook his finger at her. "I'm very sensitive to the fact that shifters do not want to be outed right now. You are suffering yourself from the fact that everyone knows you are not only an artist, but also a wolf. But don't you see how that makes you the perfect artist to create this piece? There are hundreds, possibly thousands, of other ordinary people—the kind you already feature in your work—who are secretly shifters. I have no interest in exposing them, but if you could photograph them in their shifter form and speak to how these wolves are actually people…"

Terra's whole body enlivened. "Yes! The very title— *People* of Seattle—would humanize them. It would be the contrast between the title and the image—human and wolf—that would give it life. And if a story were attached to it, the story of their lives…" She drew in a sharp breath that was excitement personified. "It would drive home their humanity."

Her cheeks were rosy, her eyes glittered, and a smile quirked around her mouth. If this was what Terra's art did to her… well, he liked it. *A lot*. She was already beautiful, and this made her come alive in a way that was singing to him deep inside.

Which only made him want to shove Julius away from her even more.

"It's brilliant!" Sally declared, interjecting for the first time. "Absolutely brilliant! Terra, my love, you *must* let me exhibit this the moment you are finished. Others will be clamoring for it, but please, I beg of you, let me be the first."

Terra's smile was lighting up the entire warehouse. "Of course. I'd be honored." To Julius, she said, "I'm in love with this idea, but it would require…" She looked over her shoulder at Kaden, doubt clouding her eyes. "It would require me getting outside, among the shifters. In the city."

Kaden was already backtracking on his assessment of

this. He shook his head. *No fucking way.* "Terra—"

"Of course," Julius interrupted him. "Your safety would be paramount. At all times. That is what your bodyguard is for, is he not?"

The sharp need to punch Julius in the face was slicing through him. Kaden barely held back. "I am not a bodyguard—"

"Or," Julius cut him off again. "Maybe this level of protection is insufficient." He gestured vaguely at Kaden but directed his words to Terra. "I'm more than happy to provide you with whatever security you need, my dear. Just let me know. If you need a battalion of armed guards, you shall have it!"

"No!" Kaden and Terra both said at the same time. She gave him a look of puzzlement, then turned back to Julius. "That won't be necessary. Besides, my subjects become uncomfortable when there's more than just me and my camera. I need them to lose themselves in their environment and their situation in order to open up to me and really reveal their inner light. I can't do that with a battalion lingering in the background." She frowned at Kaden. "Even one guard will be problematic, but I'm sure that Officer Grant is more than capable of ensuring my safety."

A warm spread through his chest to hear those words from her lips, and he had his own reasons for not wanting additional security—namely, that he didn't trust anyone else, including the other people in this very room.

"Of course," Julius said, and he didn't seem too disappointed. "I'll leave it to your discretion about the best way to create your art. But I have to say, I'm tremendously excited to see what you do with this."

Terra seemed to struggle for words for a moment… then she threw her arms around Julius's neck and hugged him. "Thank you," she said quietly. "Thank you so much for this."

Kaden gritted his teeth as Julius's hands got a little too friendly with Terra's back while returning the hug, but they broke apart before Kaden could object. Or punch something.

Fuck, he was so messed up around this. Around *her.*

His ragingly strong protective instinct aside, this whole thing was a tremendously bad idea. Once he had her alone again, he would talk her out of it. But, for the moment, he was outnumbered. And she wasn't listening to him anyway.

"Looks like we're done here?" Kaden directed his question to Terra.

She backed away from Julius, a smile on her face. "Yes, I think so. Thank you again, Julius."

"No, thank *you,* my dear." He smiled wide. "Please let me know as soon as you have any works to share. I would love to see the evolution of your process with this." He handed her a small white card with just a name and a number on it.

Terra took it and thanked him again. Kaden ushered her away, leaving Sally and Julius in the warehouse, as he shepherded Terra back through the partitions in the gallery.

"I don't like this," he said, quietly. He was leading her back toward the car. "Roaming around the city—what part of that makes any sense to you? It's insanely dangerous."

She gripped his arm, pulling him to a stop. "It makes sense because it means I can do something important with the time I have left."

Kaden squeezed his eyes shut for a moment, then open them and drilled a serious look into her deep, dark eyes. *"The time you have left?* Terra, I am not letting anyone—"

She stopped him with a raised finger. "There are no guarantees. Not of waking up in the morning. Not of living another day. Not in this life. I know you're trying to protect me, but if death is coming for me, it will find me one way or another, no matter what you do. You have to let me do this. It makes everything worthwhile."

Death was coming for her? Jesus. He was shaking his head, but he didn't have any words to fight this. "Terra, please don't do this."

Her expression softened, the anger fleeing. "I *need* to. Besides, I know somewhere safe we can go—somewhere I'll be safer than any other part of the city. Come on. I'll show you." Then she turned her back on him and strode toward the underground parking lot.

Kaden hustled after her. This was a tremendously bad idea, but he had no idea how to stop it, short of physically wrestling her into the car and driving her back to the safehouse. And she would fight that, fang and claw. Which he could handle, but still… she would complain directly to the mayor and get him pulled off this detail before he could blink.

And then she would be even worse off.

Goddammit. This was a mess.

Wherever she was dragging him off to, he would simply have to do everything possible to minimize the danger. He would defend her with his life, if he had to.

And not just because it was his job. Or because his protective instinct was in hyper overdrive. But because she was actually trying to do something good for the city and *all* its people, including shifters.

And he'd be damned if she wasn't right—that made everything worthwhile.

CHAPTER 5

Terra quickly swapped out another memory card in her camera.

She couldn't believe how much raw material she was getting. First, in the drive to the art gallery, and now, as they headed straight into one of the tougher—and more desperately alive—sections of Seattle. She'd already racked up enough shots to keep her working for weeks in her darkroom.

Officer Grant couldn't be more obviously displeased. "I really, really don't like this." He was gripping the steering wheel so hard, it squeaked under his hands.

Terra pointed her camera out the window, which was rolled down, and snapped shots as they cruised by the dilapidated storefronts and crumbling apartment buildings. They would probably be wasted shots, but she might accidentally catch something magical. Either way, it was enlivening her like she hadn't felt in months.

"Why can't you see that Julius's idea is phenomenal?" Terra asked, irritation seeping into her voice. "Is it because you're not a shifter?" She kept her gaze peering through the camera, not looking at him, but her words had to be pissing him off even more.

Surprisingly, his reply was soft. "The idea is fine. It's *you* I'm worried about."

That pulled her away from her camera.

He was staring straight ahead at the road. "We're driving into the worst possible part of the city."

She shrugged. "This is where the shifters are."

"This is where the shifter *gangs* are." The muscles in his cheek worked. "I patrol down here. I'm very aware of what *exactly* goes on down here."

She pulled her camera back into the car to face him more fully—she really didn't know anything at all about Officer Kaden Grant. "You know some of the shifters in this part of town?"

"In a manner of speaking." He threw her a slow and serious look. "First sign of trouble, and I won't care if you haven't gotten all your pictures. I'll be hauling your pretty little butt out of here—understood?"

Pretty little butt? Her wolf latched onto that sideways compliment like it was the scent of a squirrel and went bounding after it. Kaden turned back to staring at the road ahead, which was just as well because her mouth was gaping open.

She managed to shut it. "Understood."

They had almost missed where she wanted to stop. "Over here." She pointed to a parking lot that was overgrown with weeds outside an abandoned grocery store. It had been turned into a shelter of sorts—she'd never been inside, but she'd seen it during her prowls of the city. It had a not-so-secret reputation as part shifter gang headquarters and part shelter for wayward souls.

"Fantastic," Officer Grant said. This place was obviously high on his shit list.

Terra had done a lot of shooting downtown, scouring the obscure alleyways where people had been pushed to the fringes of society, but she'd kept her distance from the shifter gangs who controlled a good portion of the city… simply because she didn't want to get involved. And she hadn't actively been looking for shifters for her art before—they generally wanted their privacy kept private. But now, with this new project, the shifter gangs were *exactly* what she needed. They would benefit more than anyone else if the public could be persuaded to believe that shifters were *people*. The gangs' reputation for illicit activities and violent tendencies was somewhat earned but mostly overblown. However, they definitely operated at the margins of the city they called home—as they had to. As society forced them to. Terra knew all too well how the world simply forgot some people. She had seen more than one kind of person—shifter or not—slip through the cracks and fall down hard. Bad things could happen to anyone.

It was just like she told Officer Grant: there were no guarantees in life. She knew this from the moment her mother died, and Terra's world had been permanently darkened.

"You picked a hell of a neighborhood." Kaden had come around to open her door, and he was holding it for her to step out.

"I'm a shifter, Officer Grant. These are my people. Besides, I can handle myself." She adjusted her camera bag over her shoulder and raised her camera to her face, snapping several shots of the exterior of the run-down building. A couple of young-looking, very muscular men guarded the front door. Definitely shifters, and they were checking her out. One nodded to the other, and then he slipped inside. She knew this was more dangerous than she was letting on, but Officer Grant didn't need anything more to be agitated about.

"You may be used to roaming the streets of downtown," he said as he escorted her toward the door of the building. "But this is different. You have to know that."

She threw him a glance. How much did he know about shifters and packs? She didn't have time to ask before they arrived in front of the muscular guard at the door. He was tall, broad-shouldered, with dark brown eyes—obviously a shifter, with those muscles piled upon muscles—but with a fresh face that said he was still on the younger side of his teens.

She gestured with her camera. "I'd like to speak to whoever's in charge."

The guy folded his arms and gave her a raised eyebrow. "What exactly do you think you're going to do with that?" He flicked a look over her camera.

"My name is Terra Wilding—"

"Yeah, I know who you are." He narrowed his eyes. "Everyone does. Don't know what you're doing here, though. Seems to me like you should be leaving soon." He turned his hot glare on Officer Grant. "And we don't care for his kind here."

His kind? This kid must know Kaden was a cop.

Terra bit her lip and stared at the door, hoping someone would come soon—whoever the first guard had gone after. "Look," she said, holding out her hands to show they were empty except for the camera. "If you know who I am, you know I'm a shifter. We're on the same side."

"Doesn't look that way to me." He glared again at the hulking presence next to her.

"He doesn't have to be a part of this." Terra didn't bother glancing at Kaden—she could feel the heat of his *no way in hell* look on the side of her face.

The guard snorted his amusement, but he didn't have a chance to reply before the door swung open.

Terra opened her mouth to plead her case to whoever was in charge, but then her mouth just hung there. "Marco?" she asked, all the breath going out of her. "Oh my God, Marco Wilding! What the hell are you doing here?"

Her cousin let loose a growl, and his dark blue eyes blazed anger. "I could ask you the same thing. *Cousin.* I don't recall inviting you downtown." Then he took in Officer Grant's presence and drew back, snarling louder and letting his claws come out. That movement put the guard outside and the three other shifters accompanying him just inside the door into defensive stances.

The tension ramped up like crazy.

"What are you now, Terra?" Marco growled. "Some kind of narc?"

"What?" Terra looked between her cousin and her bodyguard, trying to figure out what was going down.

Kaden had hands up in a placating gesture. "I'm only here to protect the girl."

What the hell? "Marco!" Terra shook her camera at him. "I'm here to take pictures, not cause trouble. I had no idea you were even here. How long has it been? Ten years? I haven't even seen you since we were kids! I didn't even know you were still *alive."* The truth of that washed over her, and suddenly she found herself lurching forward and wrapping her arms around her cousin's neck.

Marco had been dark and brooding and all kinds of

trouble even when he was a kid. When he had dropped off the face of the earth, everyone assumed he'd gotten himself killed. The rebellious son of Frank Wilding, her uncle, had always been trouble waiting to happen... and it looked like he had finally found it. Uncle Frank was almost as useless as her dad, so it wasn't like he'd scoured the streets looking for his son. But when Marco went missing, it had punched her in the gut—he had always been one of her favorite cousins.

That he had been here, in the city, all this time...

It took Marco a moment, but he finally put his arms around her and hugged her back. "I didn't exactly want Dad to know where I was hanging out," he said with a wry tone of voice that made her pull back. "And I don't use the Wilding name anymore because fuck that family. Not you, Ter. The rest of them."

She nodded. They were a pretty messed up bunch. But she knew he mostly meant his own father.

She took a fresh look around. "So this is all... you? Your pack? You're in charge here?"

Marco huffed a small laugh. "Don't look so surprised."

"I'm not, it's just—"

"Whatever." He waved her off. "What are you doing

here, Ter?" His eyes dropped her camera then bounced back up again. "And *please* tell me you're mated. That you're not crazy enough to wander around shifter gangland as an unmated female." He flicked to look to Officer Grant. "Especially with *this* dumb fuck as protection."

Kaden started the growl, but it echoed all around Marco's pack.

Heat flushed Terra's cheeks—her mating status wasn't exactly something she wanted to discuss in front of Officer Grant. Or the suddenly-interested hot gazes of Marco's pack members.

She glared at her cousin. "Finding a mate hasn't been top priority—not with, you know, my family being targeted *for death*. Me in particular."

Marco's eyes flashed, but his voice quickly softened. "I know, Terra. I watch the news. And just because the family is completely fucked up doesn't mean I want to see any of them dead. And frankly, have been worried about you, especially lately. But that doesn't answer my question—why are you at my front door? Daddy finally cut you off?"

From anyone else, she would have answered that accusation with a face full of claws. But with Marco... if

Terra shocked her father out of his trance enough to cut her off... well, Marco would probably be impressed.

Instead, Terra simply raised her camera and pointed it at him, peering through the lens. "All I want is pictures. Of wolves." She fully expected him to tell her to shove off.

Marco put his hand on her lens and moved it away from his face. "Pictures of wolves? You mean shifters in wolf form. Why?"

"I'm doing a piece called *People of Seattle*... only with shifters. Starting with wolves, but I'm thinking of expanding it later. Think about it, Marco—all this fear and hatred that's running through the city. Humans think of shifters as *beasts,* not *people.* I want to show them the people inside." She glanced at the uneasy faces of the big, muscular men surrounding her. Her camera was one of the few threats that could bring that trouble to their faces. "I won't reveal anyone's identity. I just want to show the beauty of our wolf forms. I want to tell the story of your lives, the good things you do here—because I know you, Marco. I know you wouldn't be here if you weren't doing something amazing and worthwhile—I want to tie those stories, those *good* stories, to the images of wolves. Make it personal. Make it *real."*

Marco's pack had kept quiet while she spoke, and the expression on Marco's face softened. "So that's really why you're here?" he asked. "To try to change all this." He gestured to the dilapidated city around them. A small smile snuck in his face. "You always were one of my favorite cousins."

"Favorite?" she scoffed with mock outrage. "I was the only one who could put up with you."

He chuckled, but it faded quickly. "Okay. But you only shoot pictures of volunteers. And only in wolf form. And Terra—we've got more stories than you could possibly imagine here. The abused kids, the abandoned ones, the ragged halflings who don't know where else to go… we've got them all. They come to us, and they find a family. A pack. We look out for each other the way a real family should. You're welcome to come in and see who wants to take part in your project as long as it doesn't threaten any of that." Then he trained a scowl on Kaden. "But this trash stays outside."

Terra frowned, and she could sense Kaden bristling but holding back. She knew there was no way he would let her go inside a shifter gang stronghold without him. "Marco, he's my bodyguard. I can't just—"

"Bodyguard?" Marco asked, incredulously. "He's a

cop!" He said it like it was something filthy in his mouth. *"And* he's human."

"I'm in protective custody—"

"What the fuck, Terra... do you have any idea who this is?" Marco's hard glare was still on Kaden. "Do you know what he does, when he's not babysitting the mayor's favorite artist?"

Kaden lifted his chin but said nothing. The tension seemed to ramp up again.

Marco's voice dripped with disgust. "He's the worst of the worst. He *grew up* here, for fuck's sake. Born and raised right here in the dumps with us. And he couldn't high-tail it out of here fast enough. Only, you see, now he's *back*. With a shiny badge and a gun and the power to ruin lives. I can guarantee *your* safety, Terra, but no one wants the cop inside. Probably not even him."

Kaden was silent, just staring down Marco's accusations. Terra's stomach twisted. Kaden *had* said he didn't want to come here, and she had basically forced him. She didn't know what bad blood there was between him and Marco's pack, but it was obviously real and recent. Yet she couldn't leave Kaden out here alone, either. He *was* only human, and Marco's pack looked like it was just waiting for the chance to take a bite out of him.

"I'm not putting Officer Grant's life in jeopardy for this project," Terra said, firmly. "And I'm not doing this without him, either. This is about diffusing hate not feeding it."

Marco's eyes flashed again, and she knew he heard what she was saying. *That he had to take the first step of trust.* He gritted his teeth and shook his head, staring at the ground by her feet for a long moment.

Eventually, he said, "All right. *Fine.* Come on in. Bring the cop. I'll escort you the whole time and make sure no one gets overexcited."

Growls of disappointment went around his pack. He turned a sharp snarl on them, and they immediately calmed down… or at least stopped making audible sounds of disagreement. Marco opened the door and gestured them inside.

Kaden's face was inscrutable again, but Terra would bet her father's fortune that he was silently cursing her with every vile word he knew. She was asking him to take a huge risk, a *personal* risk, just for her. Worse, it was for her art… which she was sure he didn't give a flying fuck about.

"I'll make it fast," she said to both him and Marco.

And she did.

The building had been converted from a grocery store into a makeshift camp, complete with barracks, shower facilities, and a mess hall. It was half guerrilla warfare encampment and half homeless shelter. There were shifters of all ages from very young pups toddling around to aged grandmas. Terra was dying to take pictures of them in their human forms, and maybe someday she would come back here and do precisely that. But for now, she was after their inner wolves. And their stories. One by one, she explained the project, and they agreed to shift for her. Sometimes she took pictures of them on their bunks; sometimes on the floor playing with their toys. Some of the pups were so small she could practically fit them in her camera bag. Sometimes the older ones had battle wounds that were even more evident in their shifter form. In all cases, she took hundreds of shots, trying to capture that inner glow that each of them possessed, and that would bring out their true selves. She captured their stories on her phone recorder. She only stopped when she couldn't see anymore through the tears that just flowed and flowed down her face.

The whole experience was brilliant and terrible and

humbling… and by the time she left, she was completely wrung out.

Marco kept his word and kept Kaden safe. And he kept the hungry looks of the unmated male wolves from growing into something more sinister. After an intense hour, she and Kaden finally returned to the car and headed back to the safehouse.

They had survived. She'd gotten what she needed. And she was exhausted.

But she couldn't remember glowing this much in a long, long time.

CHAPTER 6

Terra had been sequestered in her bedroom/darkroom for half an hour, but Kaden was still pissed.

He knew from the start that going out—*anywhere*—was a terrible idea. The gallery was bad enough—unsecured, out in the public, meeting someone who had only been vaguely cleared. Kaden knew that clearance had legitimately come from the mayor's office... but that didn't mean he liked any part of meeting Julius. Then

Terra had insisted they go deep into downtown, right into the shifter gangland where he routinely patrolled.

He had been lucky to get out in one piece.

But what made him angry wasn't concern for his own life. It wasn't even the embarrassment of having to put himself at the mercy of shifters he was used to cuffing for dealing drugs or petty theft or more substantial crimes like that illegal car-parts ring he was sure they were running. No, the thing that still had his blood boiling was the fact that Terra had been at risk through the whole thing. It was nothing but luck that she hadn't been attacked or captured or even worse—forcefully mated.

That was something he hadn't even considered before.

Now he was all too aware that she was an unmated female... and that brought every protective instinct he had raging to the surface.

And probably clouded his judgment.

He was still coming down from the surge of adrenaline that had been coursing through his system the entire time they were out. It was like he was stuck in that mode—hyper aware, breathing hard, ready to fight. He was pacing the apartment like a trapped animal, not unlike Terra had been before they left. But she had definitely returned a changed person due to the trip. She glowed all the way back to the safehouse and had scurried immediately into her bedroom with a fist-full of memory cards. He was sure she had dived right in and probably completely forgotten about him pacing out in the livingroom. To distract himself, he tried making a sandwich, but then it just sat on the plate. He gave up after ten minutes and dumped it in the trash.

Then he went back to pacing.

He was so absorbed in his thoughts, he barely heard her door whisper open before she was light-stepping out into the livingroom, a print in her hand and a soft look of joy on her face.

His shoulders dropped. It was hard to stay angry when her art had this effect on her.

"Look at this, Kaden," she said softly as she showed him a black and white print. It was one of the little kids sitting next to the bunks they used for beds, only the kid was in his wolf form, parked on his haunches and resting his paw on a small red ball. Behind him was a half-broken, half-rusted toy truck and a book with pages falling out—the kind with big pictures and not too many words. It was cute... and at the same time, heartbreaking. Those things in the picture were pretty much all the kid had.

Kaden knew exactly how that felt.

"That's great, Terra," he said, looking away from the image. "Look, let's get something straight here. I hope you got all the pictures you need because there's no way in hell we're going back there."

Her pretty face scrunched up, and he knew that wasn't what she wanted to hear. But she didn't object, just examined him more closely, like she was looking for something. He didn't know what she thought she might find staring into his eyes, but he couldn't look away. He was supposed to keep his distance, be professional, just do his job and protect her... but it didn't work that way with Terra. She was either wide open with him or slammed completely shut—there was nothing in between. Right now she was open, and it was cracking him wide... and he was afraid of what she might see inside.

He rubbed his hand across the back of his neck and gestured toward her bedroom. "Is your darkroom working the way you wanted?"

She ignored his question. "I know you didn't want to go, Kaden. Hell, you didn't even want to leave the house. It's safer here. I get it. But nothing *happened*. It was fine. And now that I've been there once—"

"No!" He said it a little too forcefully. She pulled back, a small snarl rumbling in her chest. *Jesus Christ,* what was he doing? But that protective instinct was raging again. "Just because you didn't actually *die,* doesn't mean it was a smart idea. There're any number of ways this could've gone sideways. And there's this whole thing about you not being mated…"

Her face scrunched up more. "You don't have to worry about any of that."

He stepped closer to her and had to physically lock down his hands at his sides to keep from taking hold of her shoulders. "I have to worry about *everything.* Anything happens to you under my watch, and it's on me. You're an unmated female wolf. You're beautiful and famous. Every wolf in that gang was drooling at the idea of having you for a mate—if we hadn't run into your cousin, I don't know what you were thinking was going to happen there. As it was, the rest of them are still having fantasies about claiming you. It was just downright dangerous."

She narrowed her eyes and peered up into his face. "What do you know about wolves and mating?"

"I know enough." He ran patrols in that area—she knew that—but it went beyond that. Far beyond. But she didn't need to know the rest.

"What was all that back there?" Terra asked gesturing vaguely to the door. "Marco said you grew up there. Is that why they hate you so much? Or is it just because you're a cop, and you bust them for trying to scrape a living out of the dirty underside of our city—a city that rejects them simply because they aren't human."

"I put criminals behind bars." The growl was unmistakable in his voice. "Marco may be your cousin, but he's still running a criminal enterprise in the middle of Seattle. It's my job to put people like that in jail and protect the law-abiding citizens of the city from them."

"But you grew up there," she protested. "You know they're not all criminals."

"Yes, I grew up there. With a single mom, no father, gangs everywhere… they were pulling kids straight off the street and wrapping them up in a hopeless life of crime that would suck them down forever. I didn't have anyone to protect me. *No one*. The asshole who knocked up my mother didn't even stick around to see me born. I *escaped* that life, Terra. I only go back there now because I'm trying to save a few kids from falling into it, the way I almost did. I want to help them get out." He sucked in a breath—his chest heaved like he'd run a mile. He didn't mean to spill all that, and it left him feeling carved out in the middle. Emptied of things he never said to anyone. Not even his mother when he left her to join the police academy.

Terra's eyes had gone soft and round, and that was what really kept drawing more and more out of him.

She showed him the picture again. "This young halfling doesn't have anyone to look out for him. Marco and his gang are doing that. He rescues the halflings that no one wants—some shift; some don't, but they accept all of them. He's not doing terrible things here, Kaden. He's trying to do right by them, give them a pack. A home."

Kaden eased away from her and crossed his arms over his chest. "That's not the way I see it." She was way too close to the truth.

But rather than being put off by his words, Terra edged closer. The soft perfume of her scent washed over him—it had an essential earthy wildness to it, a pure womanly smell. It was loosening something inside him... and that something was all that was holding him back.

She reached a hand toward his face. His heart pounded in his ears, but she stopped short of touching his cheek. "What are you not telling me?" she asked, almost in a whisper. "What's your secret?"

He couldn't stop the wince, but he forced out the lie, "Don't have any secrets."

She nodded, but it wasn't like she was agreeing. "Stay right there."

What?

She dashed away, back to her bedroom. Where did she expect him to go? But in a moment she was back— she had ditched the picture and returned with her camera. She lifted it and snapped a half dozen shots before he could react.

He unlocked his arms and dropped them into fists clenched at his side. "What are you doing?"

She stayed buried behind her lens. "Tell me your secret, Kaden Grant." The camera clicked and whirred and snapped his picture another half dozen times.

"Terra," he warned.

She circled around him, taking pictures from every angle and forcing him to turn with her. He was pretty sure she was catching only his glare in her camera lens. "Terra, stop it."

She dropped the camera from her face and held it in front of her black t-shirt. "What's your story, Kaden Grant? Where's the light inside you? Every once in a while, I see something that…"

Something inside him flipped… and he moved toward her without even thinking about it. He pushed aside the camera between them. "Something that… what?"

She stared up at him with those beautiful black eyes. "Something that sends my wolf panting," she whispered.

Panting? Holy fuck. They were inches apart—too close, dangerously close—and all he wanted to do was kiss her until she couldn't breathe. Maybe even tell her the truth. She was the kind of person who wouldn't judge him. He knew that now. He half-believed her camera had already peered into him and seen the thing he wanted to keep hidden from everyone else.

"Terra." He meant it at a warning, but the growl in his voice just made her breathing hitch and her eyes dilate. He was sure she wanted him—he could scent the arousal on her. And if he got any closer, she would feel the stiffening in his pants, his body betraying him, showing what he had been thinking all along. The fact that she wasn't mated was driving him just as lust-crazed as the members of Marco's pack. He wanted to bury himself in her. Make her scream his name…

But that would be a terrible, terrible mistake.

She reached for him, and he caught her wrist. Her skin

was soft, so damn soft, and that contact almost broke his resolve. But then he slowly pushed her away and took a step back.

"My job is to protect you," he said, his voice hoarse. "Nothing more."

The room chilled ten degrees as she drew back, color flushing her cheeks—probably anger, maybe embarrassment that he let it get this far only to pull away.

"Fuck you," Terra said, soft and low but it sliced through him.

She turned her back on him and stalked back to her bedroom, slamming the door when she got there.

Goddammit. He scrubbed both hands over his face and through his hair. What the hell was he doing? His bumbling idiocy had hurt her, and that thought stabbed daggers through his chest. It shouldn't mean that much to him—*she* shouldn't mean that much to him—but somehow her anger was a live coal burning him from the inside out.

Fuck.

He staggered to the couch and sunk into it, burying his head in his hands. Even in trying not to screw this up, he'd screwed it up. But it was better this way. Better for her to be angry at him—temporarily, he was sure she'd get over it—than for them to get tangled up any further than they already were. Besides, if he took her to bed, he would have no resistance at all to whatever she wanted— he knew that much about himself. And that was no way for him to keep a clear head and keep her safe.

And *that* was the only thing that mattered.

CHAPTER 7

I t had been over an hour, and Terra could still feel the burn of Kaden's rejection.

Locking herself in her darkroom, stewing about it, certainly hadn't helped.

Kaden. He wanted her, at least physically, she could tell that much. She could scent his arousal, and the blazing look in his eyes was unmistakable... and then there had been the hard bulge in his pants that she'd only caught a glimpse of, but it had driven her wolf insane with want.

But he apparently had this idea about doing his job, and somehow that meant not getting any closer, even though he wanted to.

It was driving her crazy.

She wasn't angry at him—she was pissed off at herself. The embarrassment was almost too much, and she was drowning in the dark pain of rejection after having thrown herself at him. Rejection wasn't something she often experienced or took well, to say the very least. Yet it seemed like there was nothing but rejection in her life lately.

First, there had been Jaxson—the one alpha she thought might finally be *the one* for her, but the truth was he had never been interested, even before his mate came along and broke the spell that was holding him prisoner. Then she had shamed herself by going after his brother, Jace, as if he were some kind of consolation prize. It was just some embarrassingly desperate part of her that wanted to make Jaxson jealous.

But Jace had rejected her too.

Even her little sister had found a better mother figure, a better family, and was off on a new life without her. Never mind that Terra wanted exactly that to happen—it kept Cassie safe. But it still felt like a stinging rebuke of all the years she'd spent trying to be a mother for Cassie... and obviously failing.

And now... now even a *human male* was rejecting her. Kaden was no ordinary man, but wolf pheromones were supposed to be irresistible to members of the human race. She'd never had trouble bedding male wolves, when the itch needed to be scratched, but now she wondered if even that allure was gone...

It was like there was something broken in her.

With that dark thought, she sloshed more prints from the developer into the stop solution and then into the rinse. She had barely been paying attention to what she was doing, lost in her thoughts. When she pulled the print and turned it over, it was a complete disaster.

It was a picture of one of Marco's wolves, only washed out and bleak. Almost reversed, like a negative that put dark spots where light should be, and light had poisoned the dark.

Fuck.

She hung up the monstrous print and turned on the lights, giving up. Then she climbed up on her bed and opened her laptop—maybe there was a message from Cassie or some other distraction she could lose herself in for a while. She craned her neck, trying to work the tension from her shoulders. The heat of Kaden's rejection was still burning inside her.

A pop-up directed her to the news, so she clicked through.

What a mistake.

Her tailored news feed gave her highlights of Seattle's local news, and apparently the headlines were all about *her.*

Latest Wolf Hunter Video Attacks Local Celebrity Terra Wilding.

Jesus Lord, what now? She hesitated a long five seconds, her finger hovering over the screen, needing to know and yet dreading. This wasn't the distraction she needed. She should watch cat videos or some damn thing that would brighten her day, but no... the pull of the darkness was too much.

She clicked on it.

A new window opened with the video. It was the Wolf Hunter hiding behind his mask—this time he was wearing a Salvador Dali-esque mask, where the face was half melted on one side while still concealing the Wolf Hunter's identity. The misshapen face leered at the camera, tilting one way and then the other, then finally settling on a steady stare. The face was close enough to the camera that Terra realized for the first time—or perhaps this was the first time she could get a good luck—that his eyes were blue. Dark blue. A deep sapphire blue that was not unlike Kaden's eyes.

That thought made her shudder.

But it was nothing compared to what the Wolf Hunter did next. He leaned back and held up a large photographic print—it was one of hers. She didn't know where he got it from, probably pulled it off the Internet, but it was oversized, almost like a gallery exhibit. He ripped it in half with a long tearing sound that felt like it was pulling her apart.

"Terra Wilding." He was looking straight at her, or at least so it seemed, staring directly into the camera and right into her face. "She's the darling of Seattle, but why? Because of her photos of people in our city—*real people.* Humans! What kind of outrage is this?" He reached for another photograph and held it up to the camera—this one was an older homeless man she had photographed at the edge of dusk. He had been shivering in the cold dampness that was Seattle with nowhere to go.

"Is this how she sees humans?" the Wolf Hunter sneered. "Or maybe this is how she would *like* humans to be—downtrodden, left out in the cold, at the mercy of shifters who will prey on them in the dark alleys of our city."

He dramatically tore the photograph again and again and again, ripping it into tiny shreds and throwing them into the air as confetti. "We don't need animals like this to tell us who we are. We need to purge our city of this animal infestation." He gestured to the confetti that had fallen around him. "And Terra Wilding is a good place to start."

He leered at the camera, pulling close, and it felt like he might lurch out of the screen and grab her. She slammed the laptop shut and threw it across the room, then curled up in a ball on her bed so tight it hurt. All of her hurt, inside and out. She folded in on her stomach, which was heaving uselessly—she hadn't eaten all day, or she would be throwing it up.

Terra squeezed her eyes shut and held herself together, arms wrapped with an iron grip around her knees. It felt dangerously like she was sinking into the blackness again.

The Wolf Hunter was going to find her. And when he did, he was going to rip her into shreds just like her photographs. She'd seen the videos he made before—she didn't have to imagine what he planned to do to her. The worst was that this horror, this terror he inspired, was hollowing out everything good that happened today. All she was trying to do with her photographs. How could she hope to battle the Wolf Hunter's vile hate with a few pictures and a few stories? A child and his meager toys were nothing against that level of terror.

Minutes ticked by, then longer… she didn't know how long she sat there, curled up on the bed, but suddenly there was a buzzing sound that pulled her out of the nightmarish swirl of thoughts that had captured her mind.

She creaked open her eyes. The room was the same, of course—it could be the middle of the night or the middle of the afternoon. She wouldn't be able to tell with the window blocked.

It took her a moment to realize the buzzing was coming from her pocket. *Her phone.* She fished it out—it was a text. A small flame of hope surged in her heart… maybe it was Cassie rescuing her again, as she usually did with her life and her energy.

But it wasn't Cassie. In fact, it wasn't any number she recognized.

Hello, Terra.

It's Julius. Sally gave me your number.

If it's not too inconvenient, I would like to meet and talk about something—not in front of the others. Something a little more private.

Can you meet me?

There was no way Kaden would let her go. He wouldn't let her one step outside the safehouse, at least not today. Maybe not ever again.

But she knew a meeting with Julius was safe. And more than that, he was the one person in her life at the moment who really understood her art. She could bring some of the prints she had from this morning. Whatever he wanted to talk about didn't matter. She just desperately needed to talk to *someone* about art. About life. About something positive and growing and good—Julius was the perfect person for that.

She curled up to sitting on her bed and quickly texted him back.

Yes. Can we meet now?

Yes! Excellent.

He sent her directions to a small café in downtown Seattle. It wasn't far from the safehouse, although he couldn't possibly know where she was. She checked Google Maps and, even though it was past rush hour and close to dusk, it looked like she could take a bus from where she was and get there within twenty minutes. She texted him the time she could meet, then hurried to pluck the finished prints off the line and choose which one to bring. She didn't like showing unfinished work, so in the end, she selected only two, tucking them in a portfolio carrying case. Now... how to sneak out without Kaden stopping her? He had to be out in the living room, as he always was.

There was only one other way out... *through the window*. It was completely blocked off, but that could be undone. It might make a racket, but that would just reassure Kaden that she was still in the room—and probably keep him away, if she was tearing up her room in a fit of embarrassment or anger or whatever.

None of that mattered.

She was going to see her patron saint.

The bus ride was surprisingly quick—she was pretty familiar with all the lines from her time scouring the city for material—and she arrived downtown at the café even before her appointed time.

Julius was already there. His blue eyes were bright with shining excitement, and the fact that she was alone seemed to enchant him.

He took her hands in his. "My dear, I am so excited to

see you without your keeper. I very much appreciate you taking the time to see me, especially on such short notice."

"Of course," she said with a smile. "And I have something to show you. But you said you wanted to discuss something first—is it about my work?"

He dropped her hands, smiled, and gestured to her seat across the small table from him. It was an upscale place with white tablecloths and fresh flowers, and he seemed entirely at home. He signaled to the waiter, who quickly brought over some water. Julius instructed him to bring a bottle of red wine that Terra didn't recognize, but the waiter clearly did. He rushed off.

Then Julius folded his hands and propped his chin on them, gazing at her with a look of delight on his face. "The thing I wanted to discuss absolutely concerns your work, but that takes a backseat, if you have something to show me. I must see whatever you have!"

The glow rose up inside her again, banishing the darkness just as she knew it would. She brought the portfolio up on the table and quickly unzipped it, revealing the two prints—one of the child, the pup, and the other of an elderly woman, whose shaggy fur had silver tips like a halo all around her body.

Julius's eyes raked hungrily over the prints. "You must tell me what these are. *Please.*" The enthusiasm in his voice just fed her, loosening the tension in her body and letting the work absorb her.

"The child was born in the shelter," Terra said. "They have very little, almost nothing, but he's being raised in a pack that loves him tremendously. It's as if he has twenty fathers and a dozen mothers, in addition to the one halfling who is his actual mother."

Julius's face lit up. "A halfling?"

"Yes, someone whose parentage isn't a hundred percent wolf on both sides. It's more common than you might think. Sometimes the child will express its wolf and be able to shift; sometimes not. There are no set rules about these things, but the halfling mother mated with a full-blooded wolf, and it looks like their son is able to shift already. This brought great joy to the mother and the rest of the pack. He's a treasure. He's also apparently quite a handful."

Julius gave a small chuckle. "I can only imagine that raising a child who also can shift, complete with claws and fangs, might present a slightly different parenting challenge than normal."

Terra smiled. "Not as much as you might think—kids

are kids. It's the human side that gives the most trouble."

Julius nodded and pointed to the silver tipped shaggy wolf. "And this one?"

"She's been at the shelter for many years, more than most of the residents. Her mate was killed in some kind of violent gang rivalry several years ago. She's like the grandma for the pack now. She stays with them, helps care for the pups, and greets each new halfling or straggler or lost soul that comes through the door."

Julius was nodding again. "This is even more fantastic than I could possibly have imagined, Terra. Your work is just phenomenal here. I cannot wait until you've finished your curation."

Terra beamed. "I can't thank you enough for the idea. You've literally saved me from... well, from a darkness that's becoming more difficult as time goes on."

He frowned. "You're not talking about that monster, the Wolf Hunter, are you? Because I would hate to think that anything that maniac said was in any way influencing you."

Terra felt the darkness grabbing at her again. "Let's not talk about it, shall we? Besides, I want to hear about the mysterious thing you wish to discuss."

He examined her carefully but didn't press further

about the Wolf Hunter. "Very well, then." He leaned forward, lacing his fingers again. "I'm assuming these are not the only two wolves you have managed to procure photographs of?"

"No, I have dozens I was able to shoot this morning."

"Did you happen to see any… *white* wolves?" His blue eyes were intent on her now.

A prickle crawled up the back of her neck. "A white wolf?"

"I know they are very rare," he said. "Although our new candidate for Representative, Grace Krepky, is apparently one."

"Yes, I know." This turn was making her very nervous for a reason she couldn't quite identify. It wasn't possible for Julius to know the Wilding family had a white wolf in its past—it was just a legend in her family, until very recently when her cousin, Noah, had revealed that *he* had been turned into a white wolf by the experiments the government had performed on him. He claimed that it proved he was directly descended from the white wolf that broke up the Wilding pack to begin with, back in her grandfather's generation. Noah also said he, and the previous white wolf, were really male witches, just as the rumors that have circulated for years in her family had claimed.

Terra was as surprised as everyone else when he revealed all this. And of course she wondered, just like every other member of the family, if any of the rest of them had white wolf tendencies. She didn't shift often, but when she did, her fur was very black.

The problem was… Julius shouldn't know any of that. With the secret kept locked away, deep and dark in the Wilding pack. Had he somehow heard about Noah's revelation?

Even more importantly, why was Julius bringing up white wolves at all?

"I didn't see any white wolves today," Terra said cautiously. Which was the truth. "But I don't understand—why are you asking?"

"I know it must seem odd," he said ducking his head and toying with the tablecloth. Then he looked up. "As you may have ascertained, I have a bit of a fascination with shifters and especially those of the wolf variety. When Grace revealed that she was a white wolf, I realized there was so much more to being a shifter that I didn't understand. I investigated, doing my research, and I came across these ancient stories about the white wolf and how it was powerful. Magical. More so than the average shifter." He cleared his throat and gave her a small embarrassed smile. "Please forgive my over-exuberance. Sometimes I get excited."

"No, it's all right," she said, patting his hand. "Have you talked to Grace?"

"In fact, I have. But, of course, she knows little more than I do. It was a surprise to her to be a wolf at all! And apparently her parentage is a little bit of a sensitive topic."

Grace was mated to Jared River, Jaxson's older brother, so Terra knew the complexities involved in that whole situation. And that Grace was the bastard child of a shifter who had a fling with her mother—had, in fact, seduced her just like the hate groups like to accuse shifters of doing all the time. She could understand why Grace might not want to talk about it, especially with a human.

"Well, even though Grace is a white wolf, she's only a halfling," Terra said. "Obviously, her mother was human."

"She may only be a halfling, but she has extraordinary healing powers... or so I hear."

Terra didn't think that was necessarily secret, so she nodded.

Julius leaned forward again, looking fervent. "Don't you see? The power of the white wolf must be extraordinary. If even his halfling offspring could have such extraordinary healing powers, what must the original white wolf possess?"

The original was quite possibly a witch—but Terra wasn't about to say that. "I suppose."

"It's just a theory." Julius waved his hands around. "But I have this gut feeling… that if I can just find this white wolf, this mythical pure being, that maybe he could somehow bring peace to the city. Perhaps there's something in this white wolf that could bring us together."

Terra frowned. This idea of a white wolf being a savior… she didn't want to burst Julius's bubble about that. Besides, she didn't really have much in the way of facts—just the rumors of her family and the fact of Noah being a white wolf himself. All she really knew was that, for the Wilding family, a white wolf had left nothing but destruction in his wake.

She cleared her throat. "Well, I guess I can keep an eye out for this white wolf, if you'd like, while I'm doing my work." She hoped that would be good enough for him.

His eyes lit up again. "Excellent! And if you could perhaps ask around, as you mingle with the shifters of the city, perhaps we could piece together some clues. Any scrap of rumor or legend, anything would be helpful. It's like a grand mystery!" He looked bashful again. "It's a teeny bit of an obsession of mine, but I realize it's rather… eccentric. I appreciate your discretion in this. It wasn't something I wanted to bring up in front of the others because, well honestly, it makes me look a bit foolish. And I endeavor to be taken seriously most of the time."

That brought a smile to her face. "Your secret is safe with me, Julius."

He smiled wide. "Terra, my child, you're more of a treasure every moment I spend with you. If I were a wolf, you would be in serious danger of me asking you out on a proper date."

She grinned, but before she could respond, her phone buzzed on the table next to her.

There was no image, but she recognized Kaden's number.

Oh shit.

"Oh dear," Julius said, peering at her phone. "I hope I haven't gotten you in trouble."

She rose quickly from the table. "I'm afraid I have to go. You can keep these." She slid the portfolio and its photographs across to him.

"Of course! Of course! Run along." He waved her up and away.

She snatched up her phone and debated not answering Kaden's call at all. She knew that would be worse for her in the end, but she didn't want to take his no-doubt angry call in front of Julius.

She let it ring as she hurried out of the café.

CHAPTER 8

J *esus, she's on the run.*

Kaden was having a legit heart attack. The pain in his chest, as he stared at Terra's torn-apart window coverings, as he realized that *she wasn't fucking here*, couldn't be anything other than his heart seizing up and stopping dead still. He couldn't breathe. Couldn't think.

He'd lost her.

Fuck! No. His brain restarted as he launched across the room and shoved the dangling black drapes aside to stick his head out the window. The narrow alleyway outside the window was empty, but it dumped out onto the street. He climbed out, leaving a bent screen behind in his haste, and sprinted down the narrow passage to the front. Maybe she'd just left a moment ago. Maybe he could catch her before she got too far.

What the fuck was she doing?

He stumbled to a stop at the curb in front of the safehouse. There was no sign of her. He hurried down the sidewalk, looking everywhere, but it wasn't like he could go shouting her name through the neighborhood. They were supposed to be lying low, for fuck's sake! Kaden paced back to the front of the house, wracking his brain while he ran both hands through his hair, trying to reel in the panic enough to *think*.

Why did she leave? He raced back over their "fight"... he'd been so damn close to kissing her, sending all the wrong signals because he couldn't fucking control himself, and then, like an ass, he'd pulled back and given her some shit about just doing his job. She'd rightly told him to fuck off and stormed into her room.

In retrospect, it made perfect sense that she would bail—not "perfect sense" for a calm, rational person, but for Terra? To run off in a fit of anger? Completely consistent. And the fact that he didn't see it coming just underlined how messed up he was around her. *Completely fucking incompetent.*

And now she was gone.

He slammed a fist against his forehead. He would have time to deconstruct how much of an idiot he was later. Right now he had to find her again.

How long had she been gone? It had been over two hours before he banged on her door to check on her. Maybe she'd left right away and had time to cool down. Maybe she was wandering the streets right now wondering what the fuck to do… or worse, contemplating something truly dangerous, like going after the Wolf Hunter or some damn thing.

He pulled in a breath and blew it out through his teeth. Dammit, Kaden, *think.*

His phone.

He yanked it out of his pocket. If she were calm now, maybe he could reason with her. Talk her back in. He dialed her number, and it rang and rang… he was about to give up when she finally answered.

"Hello." It was her.

Thank God. "Jesus, Terra!" The air rushed out of him along with the relief at hearing her voice. "Are you okay?"

"Yeah. I'm okay. I... went out."

"What the—" He had to mute the phone against his chest as a string of curses burst out of him. He quickly got a grip on himself. "Where are you?" he ground out through clenched teeth.

"Kaden, I just had to—"

"Where are you?" He was on the edge of completely losing his shit. So much for calmly talking her in. *Jesus.*

"Downtown bus thirty-four." Her voice was chastened. "I'm boarding now, heading back, I promise."

"Stay on that bus." Downtown? *Fuck.* What was she doing there?

"What?" It was like she didn't think she'd heard him correctly.

"Stay on the fucking bus, Terra!" He was shouting again... so he just hung up. He had to calm the hell down, and the only way that would happen was if he got eyes on her again. He sprinted to the sedan parked under the carport next to the safehouse, climbed in, threw it in gear, and let loose another string of curses as he zoomed down the street. He couldn't peal rubber the way he wanted to—he couldn't afford to attract attention to the safehouse—but he *needed* to get to that bus.

It was a good ten minutes before he'd sped across

town and finally glimpsed Bus 34 trundling down the mainline, past shops and weaving bicycles. Kaden executed a highly illegal U-turn and came around the back of the bus. Only then did he trust himself to call her again.

This time, she picked up on the first ring. "Hello?"

"Are you still on Bus 34?"

"Yes." Her voice was quiet.

"Stay on the bus," he ordered in no uncertain terms and then hung up again.

Then he let out a long sigh, releasing some of the tension coiled deep inside him. He couldn't see *her*, but he had eyes on the vehicle. He would just tail it, watch who boarded, and make sure she stayed safe until the bus reached the stop nearest the safehouse. The vehicle was maddeningly slow and belching noxious fumes onto his car, but it wasn't much longer before they were crossing over to the neighborhood branch of the line.

When it finally reached the stop, Kaden gripped his steering wheel and watched as she scurried off. Terra didn't notice his car at first, but when the bus pulled away, she saw him glaring at her from the driver's seat. He put the car in gear and headed for the carport down the block, not stopping for her. He didn't trust himself not to make a scene, and that would attract too much attention. Her eyes were wide as he passed her, and she had damn well better get the hint that she needed to walk the final leg to the house by herself. He checked the rearview mirror. If she didn't get that pretty little ass in gear and haul it to the house, he'd double back and get her.

But she started moving.

Kaden swung the car back into the carport and checked to make sure she was still headed toward the house. She was, head down, fists at her side. He couldn't tell if she was angry or upset or what... but he was mad as hell. He was relieved to see her, and the panic had subsided, but his adrenaline was still pumping like crazy. He strode in through the front door, closed it, and waited for her just inside.

He ran his hand through his hair and tried to breathe out the stress.

She was okay. She was back. This was all going to work out.

But only if she stayed.

That thought ratcheted the tension through his body again.

The door swung open.

Terra stood in the doorway, wide-eyed and uncertain. Kaden reached for her hand on the doorknob, pulled her inside, then shoved the door shut behind her. Somehow she ended up in his arms, flat against his chest—he had a hold on her like he'd just snatched her back from drowning.

"Goddammit, tell me you're all right." He felt her head moving against him—*yes*—but that spilled her cloud of dark hair all over his hands. It worked some kind of magic on him, and suddenly he was getting lost in it, aching with the feel of her small body tucked against him. He bunched his fist in her hair and pulled her head back, tipping her face up so he could get a good look, but those big, dark eyes sucked him right in.

His mouth was suddenly on hers like it belonged there.

Her lips were hot and soft, her tongue welcoming him inside. His kiss was angry and hard and demanding, as if he was suddenly possessed, his tongue intent on owning every inch her mouth had to offer. The small whimper in her throat made his blood race. He leaned into her until he found the wall with her backside. Then his body was a cage, surrounding her, protecting her, pressing against every delicious soft curve she had. His hands found her wrists and hauled them above her head, pinning them against the wall. He could feel her heart pulse in them.

The wildness inside him wanted to *possess* her.

He gasped for air and broke the kiss.

What the fuck was he doing?

Terra's lips were swollen, her mouth hanging open from his domination of it.

"What do I have to do..." His chest heaved against hers, his hardened muscles pressing against the infinite softness of her body. "To keep you from leaving?"

Her breath caught, and her eyes hooded. Arousal mixed with the smell of hot skin and that scent that was deliciously *her*. No words were necessary. He could feel the tension quivering her body, see the need in her eyes. And all of it was turning his cock into granite.

He leaned in to whisper in her ear. "I'm going to fuck you so hard, Terra Wilding." That damn whimper again. *Jesus,* he was losing his mind with this. "You're not going anywhere for a while."

Then he plundered her mouth again, and this time, she kissed back. Reaching and biting at him. He held her still pinned to the wall as he devoured her sweetness. Then he tasted his way across her jaw and down her neck. He needed her clothes *off* fucking *now*. He released her wrists and dropped his hands to her body. One squeezed her breast hard—*fuck,* it fit perfectly in his hand—while the other cupped her ass and brought her firm against his raging erection. He enjoyed the feel of her squirming against him, hands digging into his shoulders, for just a moment… then he leaned back enough to rip her t-shirt up over her head. Her bra was a flimsy black thing with straps—he ripped it straight apart, spilling her breasts out for him to see.

"Fuck, Terra," he exhaled. "So beautiful." In an instant, his mouth was on one rock-hard nipple. Her head banged back against the wall as she arched into him. He lost his mind nipping at that bud, biting and teasing and running circles with his tongue while his hands got busy working those skinny black pants off her hips. By the time he had them down, she was moaning and writhing under the assault his tongue was waging on her breasts. She was naked before him now and so fucking glorious. He kept feasting on her while quickly undoing and shoving down his pants, freeing his aching cock. He wanted to bury himself in her, but instead, he stood tall, towering over her, and wound his hand into her hair again.

"On your knees." His hand made it clear what he

expected from her once she was there.

He half expected her to balk, to fight him—but she dropped to the floor like she couldn't wait to take him into her mouth.

"Fuck." The sight of her red, swollen lips eagerly sliding down his cock was almost as erotic as the hot wetness of her mouth taking him in. *Holy fuck…* he couldn't take too much of this without coming undone. But he kept his hand tight in her hair, directing her to take him ever deeper with each stroke. Her arousal was a cloud around him—she was getting off on this as much as he was—and somehow he knew just what she wanted. What she *needed* from him.

Hot, hard, and fast… and completely dominating.

He was so fucking ready to give that to her.

"Stand up," he commanded, pulling her sweet mouth away from his cock. *Jesus,* that was hard to do. "Turn around. Hands on the wall." He didn't wait for her to comply. She was so small and light, he just spun her to face the door and bent her forward, hands planted flat above her head and that delicious rear end sticking out to him. He reached between her legs to cup her sex, and sure enough, she was already dripping wet. He gripped her hip and drove his cock deep, filling her fast and hard from behind.

She gasped and cried out. A grunt escaped him—she was so fucking tight. Her claws came out and carved into the door, helping to hold her as he thrusted. Watching his cock slide in and out of her sweet body was almost too much—if he kept watching, it would be over in no time—so he focused on her beautiful black hair spilling and dancing along her back instead. He took her again and again, harder and faster. She was a *wolf*—as delicate as she was, she was *strong*, unlike the human women he'd fucked. He knew Terra could take any pounding he dished out. More than that, she *wanted* it. *Bad.*

He ramped up the ferocity of his thrusts and the wildness of his possession of her body against the door. Pants and moans and then cries worked out of her mouth. She was so hot and tight, shrieking his name and urging him on… he was rocketing toward a climax that was going to shatter anything he'd ever experienced. He loosened his hold on her hip to slide his hand forward, reaching to flick her clit and send her over the edge first. He could barely manage it while thrusting so deep, but his fingers found her sweet spot, and she let out a growling cry that had him exploding inside her. She pulsed all around him, squeezing him as he came so hard, he was seeing stars.

He kept thrusting through the wave of pleasure, emptying himself into her and relishing all the noise and heat and gushing wetness that joined them together. When he eased to a stop, he leaned into her, pressing her body against the door again, still joined together, still deep inside her, but now both calming their panting breaths. He caressed her breasts, her stomach, the thick mane of her hair, all from behind as he pressed his body against hers.

They slowly came down together.

It was the most intense sex he'd ever had. The limpness of her body against his said he'd taken her to that same edge and beyond. But this wasn't just sex—it was undeniably hot and erotic, but deep inside him, something was cracking loose and rising up. He was responding to her like no woman he'd ever fucked. Because that's just what it always was with other women, *human* women—just sex; a release; a pent-up need—but this was different.

Wildly different.

She was bringing out something he'd fought long and hard to keep buried.

It was this urgent need he had to protect her, to make

insanely hot love to her against the door that was doing it. All the wild passion he kept carefully locked away, contained, was coming out, wanting to claim her.

His inner beast.

It was coming alive because it wanted *her*. And because this tiny, angry, beautifully broken woman he'd just brought to orgasm *needed* him. It was more than he could resist, but he was sure she had no idea about any of it—her need, his need for her, his true nature. Terra was true to her family name, wild and unconstrained, impulsive and in need of a strong alpha to love her and keep her safe.

And he had no fucking idea what to do with that.

Especially as this hot shifter female snuggled her cute little behind against him, her body just begging for more.

He turned her around and kissed her. Softly. On the lips.

"Terra." He was breathless with all of it.

She pressed her forehead into his chest, and he held her like that, cuddling really, for a moment. Then he bent down and swept her up into his arms. She was drunk with her orgasm, her head lolling against his chest.

"Where are we going?" she asked dreamily, like she wasn't quite awake, already drifting off into a post-coital haze.

But he wasn't done with her. Not by a long shot.

"I'm taking you to bed to make love to you properly."

She blinked open her eyes and stared up at him with wonder.

He carried her into his bedroom and kicked the door closed behind them.

CHAPTER 9

Terra had just experienced the most mind-blowing sex of her life… and Kaden Grant was promising to now do it "properly."

She wasn't sure she would survive.

He was carrying her in his massive arms, but tenderly, like she was a thing that might break in his hold. The masculine scent of him was all over her, inside her, relaxing every part of her—she was *safe* with him in a way she'd never felt with any man. And certainly never with a human. That part would be blowing her mind, too, but her head was still in a cloudy haze of pleasure from being thoroughly fucked.

Made love to. He used the words, not her, but they were the last piece of the puzzle, the last bit that made her relax into the sheets of his bed as he laid her down and worshiped her body with his gaze.

He had a tattoo, a thin blue line that encircled his arm near his shoulder with the words *Protect* and *Serve* emblazoned above and below it. She knew it was some kind of police thing, but she felt like it applied directly to her. He was protecting her with his life. And he had just served her in the most delicious of ways.

Whatever Kaden asked, she would give. Without hesitation. He might even be someone she could let inside, someone she could count on... not just with her body, but her heart.

Even if being with a human was something she had never envisioned.

Kaden eased his body next to her, touching her everywhere—his knee nudging her legs apart, his hand exploring her breast, his face nuzzling her neck. Her body was instantly ready for more, craving him inside her again, although it was entirely too soon. She let her hands run free across his chest, moaning at the broad, hard-muscled expanse of it. If she weren't so busy with thoughts of lovemaking, she would wish for her camera—Kaden's body was a work of art she wanted to capture on film.

"I have to tell you something," he whispered in her ear, bringing her out of her lust-haze.

And reminding her that she had yet to explain why she'd fled out the window. "And I owe you an explanation," she whispered back, her fingers tracing a path along the rippled muscles of his chest around to his back.

He brushed her hair from her face and peered into her eyes. "You first."

She swallowed, feeling foolish now about leaving without telling him. In fact, she couldn't imagine keeping anything from him now. "I met with Julius."

Kaden winced, and her fingers immediately went to the crease in his brow, smoothing it. "I should have told you."

"Yes, you should have." His eyes blazed, and that sent a thrill through her. His soft caresses turned suddenly hard. He slid an arm under her knees and lifted them, folding her up with her knees practically to her chest and exposing her bare bottom. Then his other hand came down, spanking her hard. The sting of it shot pleasure straight to her core, but her mouth fell open in shock. He spanked her again, fast and hot against the other cheek, then he leaned in to whisper with a full smirk, "A little reminder that you should always tell me first."

His spanking hand was now sliding over her bottom, soothing it, although the sting was already gone.

She swallowed, her mouth suddenly dry. "That might have the opposite effect."

His eyes blazed again, but his hand moved to her sex this time, quickly sliding two fingers inside. She gasped and gripped his shoulder, the one she could reach around her folded legs. He started pumping her with his hand, and she squirmed against him, wanting more and quickly starting to pant. *God,* he could take her from zero to sixty in two spanks and two strokes.

"I thought you had something to tell me," she gasped, trying and failing to keep the moan inside. He was plunging deeper now, flicking her clit once with every stroke. *Goddamn,* he was a *god* in bed, and not just with his gorgeous body, but the way he played hers to perfection.

"It can wait." His voice was tight, and as he pulled her closer, she felt his erection gaining strength against her newly-spanked bottom. "I'm not done with your punishment yet."

Oh god. Her core clenched around his fingers with those words, and she nearly came.

But there was no more spanking in store. He just eased up to his knees, drawing her legs up until her ankles rested on his shoulders. His hand still plunged inside her, but now his cock was fully erect, on display between her splayed legs. She reached for it, stroking it, and his hand answered with even more thrusting. She had to resist arching up with the pleasure he was giving her, because she would lose her grip on him... she quivered at the thought of having his cock inside her again. He was so large, so thick and long and strong, the feel of it pulsing in her hand was making her whimper. When she'd had it in her mouth, she could only take a fraction of him. When he'd taken her from behind, he'd stretched and filled her like no man ever had.

He pulled her hand away from his cock, causing her to make an ungracious sound of protest.

"Kaden, *please.*" She was begging him, and it seemed to only spark the fire in his eyes.

"Oh?" he teased, leaning forward. Her legs were still over his shoulders, only now he was face-to-face with her, and her ankles were up by her ears. She was nearly folded in half, with his cock poised at her entrance. "Do you want me, Ms. Wilding?"

Oh, my god. "Yes," was all she could manage, her eyes wide with the prospect of taking him so deeply in this position. She clutched at his back, trying to draw him into her, but he held back. If he weren't human, she would let out her claws to show him *exactly* how much she wanted him inside her.

His cock nudged her, teasing her. "All of me?"

"Oh my god, Kaden." She arched up into him, but he moved to prevent himself from sinking into her.

Then he kissed her tenderly on the lips between her gasps of want. "Say you want all of me."

"I want all of you," she said in a rush.

He eased a little inside her—only a little, but it made her gasp.

"Say you'll stay," he whispered in her ear. "Say you'll let me keep you safe."

"I'll do anything you ask," she gasped. *And she meant it.* Not just because she wanted his cock inside her *now*... but because her wolf was whimpering desperately for him, proclaiming that this man was the alpha she'd been waiting for.

"Yes, you will," he said, hoarsely. Then he thrust his cock inside her, *hard*… and so deep, she shrieked.

He moaned and stayed deep, not moving. "God, Terra," he said, eyes shut with the pleasure. Then he opened them and held her gaze with his dark blue eyes blazing. "I want you like this… *forever.*"

Her wolf leaped for joy, but her heart barely had time to register what he'd said before he pulled back and thrust again, hard and deep. And then he was pounding into her, and no other thoughts were possible. Before, when Kaden had her up against the wall, she had been lost in the pure, insane pleasure of it… and he had seemed in control, distant and erotic. Now, with him deeper inside her than any man had ever been, he was face-to-face with her and breathing hard, moaning and swearing under his breath as he plunged again and again. His face was twisted in sweet torment, and it doubled her pleasure knowing she was giving so much to him.

"Goddamn it, Terra," he said hoarsely. "I need you to come for me." He shifted his angle a little, and then her vision whited out as he hit a new spot that rushed her to the edge. She screamed his name, again and again, clutching at him, and then the rising wave of pleasure broke—and she bucked so hard, her mind blotted out, and she wasn't even sure where she was anymore. She was lost in loving and being loved, an endless sea of pleasure drowning her. Kaden roared and buried himself deep, holding still as he pulsed inside her. That stretched a long moment, and then they rocked a little more, riding the wave as it settled, until Terra literally had no energy left at all.

She sank into the sheets, utterly limp and spent.

Kaden pulled out, unfolded her legs, then drew her up next to him, the length of his amazing body pressed against hers, tucking her smaller form into the vast safety of his.

"Good God, woman," he breathed into her hair. "I want to do that to you again. Very, very soon."

Her heart swelled. Could he really mean this? Was he really saying these things to her? And did it mean what she thought? Because for humans, all of this had to be so different. For wolves, there was mating—a literal magical bond that held them together. If she had this kind of experience with a wolf, those words would mean: *you are my mate*. They would both know. Her wolf and his would be singing to each other. She almost had that with Jaxson, although she never got close enough to him to find out if her wolf's whimperings were justified. If he was truly for *her*. And it turned out, he wasn't.

But with humans… what did all of this mean?

She cuddled into his chest as those thoughts rumbled through the post-climax bliss that was still buzzing her body. She couldn't even begin to know how to talk about this with him.

Kaden was quiet for a minute, just stroking her hair and breathing it in. Then he said, "Terra, I need to tell you now before this goes much further."

Her heart seized up, but she forced herself to pull back and meet his gaze.

It was so tender, it almost broke her heart.

He ran a thumb along her cheek. "God, you are so beautiful."

She smiled. "Is that really what you wanted to tell me?"

He frowned. "No." Then he struggled for a moment, and said, "I have a secret. No one knows. Like, literally *no one*. But I have to tell you because… because of this." He let his gaze drop to her bare breasts pressing against his chest.

She just nodded, afraid to speak.

He swallowed. "Everyone thinks I'm human… but I'm not."

Her eyes went wide. "You're a *wolf*."

He gave a small nod.

A smile burst across her face. "I *knew* it!" She pushed him back on the bed and climbed on top of him. His eyes went wide as she straddled him and slapped both hands down on his chest. "I *knew* you were an alpha! My wolf has been singing it from the moment I saw you!" The joy was practically bursting out of her.

Kaden caught her wrists before she could playfully beat on him again. There was no smile on his face. "No one can know, Terra. No one."

Her smile dimmed. "Why not?" But her brain was already ticking through the implications. He worked for the Seattle Police Department—a *human* police force. "Would the SPD fire you?" She scowled. Dammit, that was so wrong, it just twisted her up inside.

He frowned. "Probably. Even if they didn't... I'd have to watch my back every minute. You know how they are."

She leaned back, shoulders slumping. "You can't come out because they hate wolves."

He winced. "Let's just say there's a reason I tried so hard to get this assignment."

Her eyes narrowed. *He did?* She could have sworn he

hated it from the moment she saw him... her eyes went wide again, and she leaned forward, her hands resting on his chest. "You were trying to protect me. *From them.*"

He nodded.

Her heart had that swelling feeling again. She slid her hands up around his neck, moving skin-on-skin against him and purring when that wrenched a small groan out of him. Her wolf strutted, validated in her assessment of Kaden. From the beginning, he was drawn to help her. *Protect her.* Before he even knew her. Before he knew anything other than what the public could see. And that was *exactly* how it was supposed to happen with mates— they were drawn to each other, the forces of the universe conspiring to bring them together at the perfect moment, when they needed each other most.

When death was about to catch up to her, finally, her true mate had appeared.

His hands were roaming his body. "Jesus, Terra." His voice was hoarse again. "All you have to do is touch me, and my wolf comes alive, wanting to claim you again and again."

She pulled back, unable to restrain the smirk of satisfaction. "That can very much be arranged." Holy shit... normal sex with Kaden was *amazing*—how much better would mating sex be?

But he was back to scowling again. "I'm not a good match for you, Terra."

What? The smile died on her face. She smacked his chest with her open palm. "What the hell are you talking about, Kaden Grant?"

He raised his arms in defense, and a small smile quirked on his face, then quickly fled. "I'm in *hiding,* Terra. What are you going to do, mate with someone who's supposedly human? That's not even mating, and you know it. Everyone will know it. There's no way anyone would believe someone like *you* would choose to be with someone like *me.*"

She scowled and climbed off him, drawing her knees up and locking her arms around them. "I don't know what you mean." But she did. Even worse, she knew it could never be kept secret. She was too high-profile. The gossip pages would be all over her. The rumors alone would basically out Kaden as a wolf, even if he never admitted it.

Mating with her could *ruin* him.

Kaden rolled up to sitting next to her. He gently swept her sex-tossed hair behind her shoulder. "I would give my life to protect you. I would give up the force, my job, anything… just to have the honor of being with you and keeping you safe. But I would *have* to come out as a wolf and… well, my wolf isn't the kind you're going to want as a mate."

She frowned again. He wasn't concerned about *himself*… he was concerned about *her?* "I don't understand."

He sucked in a breath. "I'm just a halfling, Terra. My mother was human. And my father was the kind of wolf who got off with a human and then split. He was an asshole who didn't care where he spread his seed or what halflings he left behind." Kaden raked his gaze over her still-naked body. "Didn't you wonder why I didn't bother with protection? Or even ask?"

Her eyes went wide. She was so used to being with wolves, it didn't even occur to her. But of course, a human wouldn't know…

Kaden nodded. "I learned early on how to scent women—human and shifter. Although you're the first shifter I've… well, the first one I've made love to. But I would never have if you were in your fertile time. I don't want to be an asshole like my father."

She unlocked her arms and placed her hands on his shoulders. "You are the extreme opposite of whoever that guy was."

He scowled. "I don't know about that. I have his DNA. And it's fucking strong. I may only be a halfling, but I can shift. And, well, there's something unusual about my wolf form." He gritted his teeth. "Let's just say I'm sure there are full-blooded alphas out there who would be much better mates for you." Then he pressed his lips shut, and it looked like he was ready to kill something.

Which is exactly how she felt about mating with anyone else.

Her wolf was growling at the thought and demanding that she do something about it. And Terra wholeheartedly agreed. She slowly slid her hands down Kaden's well-muscled chest. He gave her a look that was both chastising and thick with lust. She reached his cock, which was spent from their lovemaking, and grasped it hard, giving it a good stroke.

Kaden squirmed. "Jesus, Terra—" But his cock came unmistakably alive in her hand.

She grinned and stroked him some more, bringing him erect in no time flat. Then she sidled her body up to his, her breasts in his face, enticing him. She stopped tormenting him with her hand and wrapped her arms around his neck, taking a moment to stare into his eyes, her smile fading into seriousness.

"You are my alpha," she said with all the reverent joy in her heart. "You will always respond to my touch more than any other woman on this planet. I am meant for you, and you are meant for me. And I don't want to hear you talking about any other mates because that's *not* how it's going to be."

His hands were suddenly in her hair, bringing her down for a kiss that devoured her and made her heart fly again.

When he released her, his voice was rough. "Is this how it always is?" he asked, breathless. "Is this how it is with mates? I've heard the stories, but... I'm losing my mind around you, Terra."

"Damn right, you are." She kissed him again, long and deep. When she broke it, she gave him another solemn look before saying, "I need you, Kaden Grant."

His expression softened. "You have no idea what that does to me."

If it was anything like it was doing to her... "I need more than just your body. I need your magic. I need to submit to you. To my alpha."

He blinked. "I've never..." He swallowed. "I stayed

away from the gangs, Terra. They don't even know I'm a... I haven't shifted in *years*. I've never submitted to anyone. I'm not even sure how..."

She grinned wide. "Shift for me, you big baby."

He growled a warning at her, looked uncertain for a moment, then released her to move back on the bed. Another uncertain look, then he shifted...

Into a white wolf.

Terra's hands flew to her mouth, covering it while it gaped open. No fucking way. "You're... I can't believe it. You're a *white wolf.*"

He shifted back, naked and scowling on the bed. "I told you there was—"

She scrambled across the tangled sheets to him. "No, no, no. Don't misunderstand. It's... *glorious.*" She smiled as she cupped his cheeks. The scowl disappeared from his face. "It's just... there are some things you should know about that."

He frowned. "Like what?"

"First things first." Her smile beamed. No way would she let him out of this room before she flushed him full of the magic that a submission would bring. And submitting to a white wolf... if he were really part-witch like her cousin, Noah, the submission would be a little bit dangerous and wild and… she was getting hot just thinking about it. "Shift back into that gorgeous wolf form. My wolf is dying to meet you."

This time, there was no hesitation. He shifted right in front of her. She smiled and shifted as well. They both were standing on the bed now on all fours. She immediately went for the submission pose—furry paws stretching out in front, rump in the air, head dipping down, tail tucked. Kaden may not know much about submission, but his wolf did. Her pose drew out the alpha in him, and he quickly stood tall, ears forward, tail held high. As soon as they both were in the pose that induced the magic, it washed over her like an electrical storm, enlivening her, building her up even as it bound her to him. Until at least the next full moon, he was her alpha in fact, in magic, not just in destiny. The bond had to be bolstering him, flushing him full of magical energy as well. Her submission would literally make him stronger. And he would protect her with his life, just as he promised. She was now *pack* with him. She would serve him, and soon enough, she would seal it with a mating bond.

But not just yet.

Kaden needed to understand more about his wolf.

And she knew just what to do about that, too. The thrill of being able to introduce him to it, to guide him in his assumption of his true alpha form, had her wriggling in her submission pose, eager to make love to that gorgeous human body again.

After a moment, she realized he probably wasn't used to communicating via thoughts. Or knew the proper protocol to release her from the submission pose.

My love, she sent a thought to him.

Holy shit. His thoughts were a rambling mess, uncontrolled. *Oh, right. This is a pack thing, right? This thought thing? Holy shit.*

Her wolf was chuckling in little wolfy yips.

Are you fucking laughing at me, Terra Wilding? He was actually a little steamed.

She still had her head ducked in the submission position, so she couldn't quite see his expression, but she could sense his emotions in his thoughts. *No, my love. But I'm yours now. You have to give the command for me to rise and shift, or I'll be stuck with my rump in the air all day.*

Oh. Um. Uh…

There must be some secret alpha handshake that passed these things on. And her alpha had never received his training.

Just tell me to 'rise,' my love. She restrained her laughter because her alpha deserved more compassion than that.

Rise, my love.

She popped up instantly and nuzzled him. Did he really just call her 'my love?' It wasn't necessary to release her, but maybe he thought it was? She didn't care—she just loved hearing it.

This feeling... His thoughts were still full of wonder. *Did the submission hurt you? I feel energized, like I must have stolen something from you, maybe some of your magic...*

No, my love, she thought, licking his face. And seriously wanting to lick other parts, but in her human form. *The bond lifts us both. And this is just submission...* Mating would be a hundred times more wondrous and intense. But she didn't want to talk about that yet.

You have to tell me to shift, she sent the thought to him.

Shift, my love, he sent the thought quickly.

She did, and a moment later, she was skin-on-skin with him, enveloped in his arms as he covered her body with his. His erection was back, as she suspected it might be—submission energized more than just a man's magic—and her deliciously sore nether parts were already quivering in anticipation.

"That was amazing," he breathed, gazing into her

eyes.

Her hands roamed his face. "I can't believe I've found you." Then she had to stop because she was choking up a bit. "I didn't know if I ever would."

His eyes took on a fierce look. "This bond between us… it's making my wolf *stronger*."

"That's the magic of the submission." She bit her lip. "It enhances… everything."

"Everything?" he asked, eyes roaming down to her chest.

She could feel his hunger like a hot stroke on her skin. "Oh yes," she breathed.

He dove in, nipping and tasting her, touching her everywhere. Her wolf leaped for joy.

There was so much he needed to know—about mating, about his white wolf, about *her*.

But it could wait just a little longer.

CHAPTER 10

K aden wasn't at all sure this was a good idea.

It was morning, and he and Terra were driving back up to the River pack's mountain estate, the one where he originally picked her up before he brought her into safekeeping. She wanted him to talk to her cousin, Noah, about being a white wolf, but all Kaden could think about was how unsecure the location was… and how little interest he had in talking to any wolves other than her.

"Well, this is a nice scenic drive through to

mountains," he said to Terra in the passenger seat next to him. "How about we return to the safehouse now?"

"Noah's expecting us. We're lucky he's still there with his mate." She scowled at him, but there was no heat in it… just the glow left over from an entire night of lovemaking. After literally hours of tearing up the sheets, he'd legit needed a rest and a shower—which they both got—but they were both still floating on the magical high of the submission bond and the sex.

Good God, the sex. He would much rather have stayed in seclusion with nothing but Terra and a bed, than go on this road trip to awkward. He still was coming to grips with the fact that his wolf was fully resurgent after years of suppressing and denying and generally keeping that shit locked up. He was *not* thrilled about discussing the strange nature of his beast with anyone, much less a man he didn't know.

"Your cousin's fancy mountain estate isn't exactly *safe,* Terra," Kaden complained, not giving up. They would be there in just a few minutes. "The Wolf Hunter knows that location. Hell, everyone with access to the internet does. I'll pull over here, and we can call him."

"No." The scowl was definitely darkening. "You need to shift for him… and him for you. You need to share things. I'm not even going to be in the room."

"What?" Kaden's wolf surged up with that, and he had to grip the steering wheel to keep it under control. When Terra had submitted to him, it had truly brought out his inner alpha… and he was still having trouble keeping it contained. Now that it had been awakened, it was raging under his skin, which also brought out his primal protective side. Anything that smelled like a threat to Terra—including letting her out of his sight at the estate—surged up a huge helping of *fuck no* growling in his chest. "Where do you think you're going to be?" he asked her.

She threw out her hands like he was hopeless. "I'll be upstairs in my old room."

"I don't like it." His head was buzzing with growls. He could barely think straight, but then his wolf was a fucking beast… not a man. Kaden sucked in a breath through his teeth. He needed to get this under control.

Terra seemed to sense his need to calm down—she scooted over and leaned her thin frame over the console between them. One hand gripped his bicep and squeezed while the other slid to the back of his neck and played with a short scruff of hair.

It worked. Just having her close ramped down some

of the tension.

"I'll be right upstairs," she whispered in his ear. "Waiting for you to get done with your business. Then we can explore a few new positions I've been thinking about…"

Jesus. His pants were tightening already. "Unless you want me sporting wood for Noah, you'd better keep those thoughts to yourself."

She grinned, and he nearly pulled over for a little relief by the side of the road. But they were almost there anyway.

She scooted back to her side of the car. "Take your time with Noah. I've got a few things to pack up that got left behind before, and I'd like to call my family."

"All right," Kaden said, finally giving up. "But the sooner we're back at the safehouse, the happier I'll be."

She beamed at him. "If there's one thing I want, it's to make you happy."

"Terra," he warned. For the love of God. She was beautiful and amazing and perfect for him… but the constant need to *have* her, to be buried inside her, to be making wild love with her, just might kill him.

She giggled, and that did *not* help matters.

Thankfully, she got serious again. "Before you go in,

there's something else you should know."

"Something more than the fact that your cousin is a strange white wolf like me?" It was still unsettling to him that there was *another* white wolf out there. "Between Noah, me, and Grace Krepky, we could start a White Wolf Club." Krepky was the first openly-shifter candidate for the House of Representatives. When she came out to the world, that's what tipped off all this hate-group business. And it freaked him out a little, given he knew his wolf was white as well, even if he hadn't seen it in years. Kaden knew plenty of wolves in the gangs. He'd grown up around them. He always thought white wolves were legends...

Until he shifted and realized he *was* one.

"Something more strange than that," Terra said, her voice serious. "When I met with Julius, he wanted to talk to me privately because, apparently, he's obsessed with white wolves."

"Really?" Kaden frowned at her as he pulled into the gravel parking area in front of the River estate. "Okay, that's odd."

"Yeah," she said, frowning as well. "I thought at first he somehow knew about the Wilding family secret."

Kaden put the car in park and turned to her. "Family

secret? Other than the fact that you're all wolves?" Which wasn't exactly secret anymore. He didn't say that part.

But she still genuinely seemed distressed.

"Hey." Kaden reached over and stroked the hair framing her face. "Whatever it is, I'm already tumbling down a steep hill, falling in love with you. So, unless you're all mafia or something, I'm pretty sure it won't change anything between us. And probably not even then."

She gazed at him with those dark, beautiful eyes, and he could feel it again—that unsteady, falling feeling he'd had since he'd first laid eyes on her. "The Wilding pack was broken up by a feud between my grandfather and his brother. Turns out, his brother slept with his mate."

Kaden ground his teeth. "Sounds like an upstanding guy."

"It broke up the family," she said, "but here's the kicker—the brother was a white wolf."

Kaden dropped his gaze. "Great. So, pretty much all white wolves are assholes."

"*No.*" The ferocity of her word made him look up. "Noah's not. Grace isn't. You're definitely not! But it did make me wonder. My grandfather's brother screwed his alpha's mate. Grace is the halfling product of an affair her mother had with a white wolf. And you…"

Kaden narrowed his eyes. "And my mother was bedded by an asshole white wolf. Who then took off."

"And Grace is about the same age as you." She nodded, slowly, like she wasn't sure how he would take this. *He* wasn't sure how to take it.

"You think Grace Krepky might be my half-sister?" He blinked and leaned back. *Holy shit.* But then again… it made a weird kind of sense. If his asshole father went around bedding human woman, he probably did it more than once.

"Maybe." She bit her lip, and he could tell there was more.

"What?" he asked.

"It's possible it's the same guy." She winced. "The same Wilding white wolf who broke up my pack."

His eyes went wide at that. *'What?* Wait… your grandfather's brother? That's… that doesn't make any sense, Terra. He'd have to be dead by now. Or ancient. Or some shit. Not going around seducing women twenty-one years ago."

She slowly shook her head. "Except… maybe he did. Maybe he didn't ever actually get old."

"What are you saying?"

"There's one more thing you should know about him." Her face scrunched up like she was afraid to say it.

"And that is?"

"He's probably a witch."

His mouth went dry. "A witch. A male witch. And you think… you think that I might be…" His mind blanked out. He'd dealt with witches on the force—they were often brought in to handle shifters in custody—but they were all women, seductive as hell, and not a single damn one was a guy. But they were all preternaturally beautiful… and didn't age a bit. "I don't… *Jesus,* Terra, what are you even saying here?"

Her thin shoulders quivered a little. "I'm saying Noah's a white wolf. And part witch. And you should probably talk to him about that." He could tell it was freaking her out just to say those words.

His wolf surged up, demanding that he protect her, soothe her, do *something* to stop that quivering and get rid of the frightened look in her eyes. At least he thought it was his wolf demanding those things… suddenly the world didn't make any sense at all.

Except that Terra was looking at him like she was afraid and that had to stop *now.*

He reached out and pulled her small body from the

passenger side, over the gap between their seats, and into his lap. He smoothed back her hair, cupped her cheek with one hand, and kissed her gently.

"Okay, I'll go talk to your cousin," he said softly. "And I'll try to figure out what the hell I am. But I don't care what happened a million years ago in your family. And I don't care who my father really is. All I know is that you complete me, Terra Wilding. Nothing else matters to me."

Her eyes glassed a little, and she buried her head in the crook of his neck, hugging him hard. He held her tight, giving her the strength of his body until the shaking in hers subsided.

When she finally pulled back, she said, "I knew you were strong enough to handle this... whatever it ends up being. You're nothing like your father, no matter who he is. You're not the kind to run or cave in when things get tough. Not like my father." Those last words were so soft, Kaden almost didn't hear them.

"You're father?" he probed gently. "I know your mother died a long time ago." At her surprised look, he just gave a small smile. "I read up on you before I took your case."

"I see." She seemed both pleased and perplexed by

that.

He pressed on. "But I thought your father was still around."

"Only in the literal sense." She sighed, and her fingers moved deliciously at the back of his neck. "When my mother died, he checked out completely. Trent and Cassie and I… we pretty much raised ourselves."

A growl rumbled deep in his chest. This… *this* was why she needed him. This was the pain he'd sensed in her, that she carried around like a rock tied to her neck. "I'll always be there for you, Terra. You can count on me." And that was a promise he had no problem making. Any threat to her felt like it was tearing him apart. That was doubly true now that she had submitted to him. He couldn't imagine how strong the feeling would be if they were mated. He still wasn't convinced that was the right thing for her to do, but he was pretty damn sure there would never be anyone else for him, regardless.

"I know." She kissed him, once, twice… then the third one got a little hotter. Her hands were bunching up his t-shirt, his cock was already springing to attention, and if she didn't stop that, he was going to haul her into the back seat and sink himself into her delicious body again. He'd lost track of how many times they'd done it in the last dozen hours… but it would apparently never be enough.

Around her, he was insatiable.

He pulled her arms from their hold on his neck. "Baby, I want you like I want air to breathe… but it's going to be really fucking embarrassing to meet your cousin when I'm hard as a rock."

She sighed her disappointment. "All right. I did haul you up here, after all. But I swear to God, Kaden Grant, we need to be mated, and soon. I'm dying to have you sink your fangs into me."

His mouth went dry again. Not that he didn't want to… he just wanted to make sure it was something Terra really wanted. And they were moving at fucking *lightspeed* with this relationship. It was flat insane. Every cautious element in his cop-brain was saying *slow down you fucking idiot,* but the beast inside him was having none of that.

Or possibly his inner witch.

Fuck.

Terra was right—he needed to sort that out before they went any further.

"Let's go see your cousin," he said, wrenching her off his body to give his cock a chance to cool down. Then he had some serious questions for Noah Wilding.

CHAPTER 11

Terra was back in her old room, but it didn't feel like a prison any longer.

She left Kaden downstairs facing off with her cousin, Noah, each of them young and tall and broad and silent. Kaden didn't like the idea, she knew that, but she had utter confidence that he would face this inner demon that had been chasing him his entire life. He'd never had another wolf to depend on, much less an entire pack, and that was something her future mate deserved—he was the kind of man who was strong enough to be a lone wolf. He'd done it on his own since he was a child. And that took a special kind of inner strength. She knew he could handle whatever Noah had to say about being a white wolf... and possibly a witch.

Although Terra was still a little dazed by it herself. She'd always assumed her perfect mate would be a wolf, through and through. An alpha's alpha. But Kaden was definitely her mate, and his white wolf made a strange sort of sense... it had a witch's power and a wolf's inner light. He was even *stronger* than the most alpha of alphas. It would be hard on him to sort this out, but she trusted Kaden to lead the way forward. He was the kind man she could follow.

She just needed to keep herself busy for a while, to give Noah and Kaden some time to figure it out.

Her brother, Trent, had packed up most of her things already—she just had a few odd-assortment lenses and specialty papers left in the room. It wouldn't take long to box them up. But first, she had someone she needed to call. And it wasn't her family... she wasn't looking forward to that, not with the news she had to share.

She scrolled through the contacts on her phone and found the number for Grace Krepky. Terra had no idea if Grace would even accept her call—she was an important person now, touring the state with her mate, Jared River, as she campaigned for Representative. Jared rarely left her side, keeping her safe from the haters, as a mate should. In a way, Terra could relate to Grace—they were both in the public eye—but Grace had another whole level of bravery that Terra did not possess. The woman had voluntarily outed herself as a wolf and was actively campaigning for equal rights for shifters—at a time when it seemed like the entire city of Seattle was against them. Terra hid behind her camera lens, trying to do something good with the result, but Grace was the true hero.

The call went through, and someone picked up. "Hello?" It was a woman.

"Is this Grace Krepky?"

"Terra Wilding?" Grace must've read her caller ID. "How are you holding up, hon? Jared's been telling me all about your family and how they had to leave the safehouse and scatter to the winds. Are you all right?"

Terra flushed with a kind of embarrassment—Grace was worried about *her?* With everything else going on? "Yeah, I'm fine. I hope you don't mind me calling. I just had a question for you, but if you're too busy…"

"I'm never too busy for anyone in the Wilding or River packs." There was a shuffling noise, like she was covering the phone with her hand, then the sound of a door closing. "Truth be told, you just rescued me from an excruciating meeting on polling statistics. Now, please, keep me occupied for the next half hour or so."

Terra had to laugh. And that alone amazed her—the giggles, the laughs, the bubbly feeling of joy—all of it was *Kaden*. It was like the mere presence of her future mate had banished the darkness that had haunted her entire life.

"Well, I'll keep you as occupied as I can," Terra said. "I've got a few things of my own that I'm trying to avoid dealing with."

"I always knew we should be friends, Terra." There was a smile in her voice. "Now, what was that question you wanted to ask?"

"Have you ever met or spoken with an art collector named Julius McGovern?" Terra asked. "He has a peculiar interest in shifter art… and he mentioned your name." Terra didn't want to spill the part about Julius's interest white wolves just yet. And she definitely wasn't revealing Kaden's secret until he had cleared her to do so. But Grace would know what she meant if she'd actually spoken to Julius.

"Doesn't ring a bell," Grace said. "But I've talked to

so many people in the last few months, all over the state, I honestly couldn't tell you."

Terra frowned. "This is a conversation you would remember."

"Oh? Why would that be?"

"I can't really say right now, but why would he claim to have talked to you, if he hadn't?" Terra didn't like the implication. Why would Julius lie? Or was he just exaggerating his importance somehow? Hobnobbing with the politician?

"Well, don't indict this Julius person yet. I have the world's worst memory. It's a terrible handicap when you're meeting thousands of people over a very short period of time. Honestly, I'm really not cut out to be a politician." Grace sighed over the phone.

"Well, you're more cut out for it than I am, that's for sure," Terra said. "I've been locked up in hiding forever—"

A knock at the door cut her off.

Terra shuffled toward it. "Hey, Grace, can I call you later? I'm sorry, but someone's at my door. And there aren't too many people here at the safehouse anymore. It's probably important."

"Of course! Go—but we should talk again soon. Take

care, Terra."

"You too." Terra clicked off her phone, but when she opened the door, the last person she expected was there.

Mama River.

That didn't stop Terra from throwing her arms around the older woman. She didn't seem the least bit surprised by Terra's overenthusiastic greeting.

Mama River returned her hug. "My child, you're back! When I heard, I came straight away to talk to you." She released Terra but then held her cheeks with fingers that were thin and cool to the touch. "I expected to see the toll all this has taken on you," she said, peering into Terra's eyes, "but there's more light in your eyes than when you left. What has happened, my child?"

"I've found my mate." Terra hadn't meant to spill it like that, but it just gushed out of her.

Mama River released her and quirked up both eyebrows. "Well now, that *is* something that will perk someone right up." Then she frowned again. "But it's only been a few days, Terra, and you've been secreted away in police custody—where on earth did you find this mate of yours?"

Terra's joy dimmed with the reminder that Kaden worked for the Police Department... and that was just one of the obstacles they would have to overcome.

Terra bit her lip and held Mama River's concerned gaze. "My mate is Kaden Grant."

If the woman was surprised before, now she was flat-out shocked. *"The cop?* The one in my living room talking to Noah?"

Terra nodded. "He's a wolf. A *secret* wolf." Terra couldn't say anything about the white wolf part of the equation, but him talking to Noah should be a clue. "We're not mated yet, but I know he's the one, Mama River. I just..." She hesitated, not sure how to even express her worries.

Mama River's expression softened. "What's troubling you?"

"If we mate, Kaden will be outed as a wolf. Being with me will mean he can't be a cop. I'll *ruin* his career. I have money—more than enough—but that's not what's important in life. He needs to have his own calling, and I'm not sure what that is. I've really just met him and yet... I feel like I've known him forever. He's the one I've been waiting for my entire life! I just... I want to make sure I'm not the thing that ruins *his.*"

There it was—she trusted Kaden to find his own way with his inner wolf/witch, but she was afraid that the way he was drawn to her might not be the best thing for him.

Mama River shook her head in slow chastisement. "The most important thing in any wolf's life is to find their mate."

Terra knew that was true, but she still worried.

The woman's cool hands landed on her shoulders again. "Once you have found each other, the rest you can figure out. *Together*. When Papa River was around, he was all that mattered to me. We had our ups and downs, like anyone else, but we had each other. And then we had the boys, and the rest we figured out together. And let me tell you something—anything I thought was a challenge before, during our time together, was absolutely nothing compared to the challenge of losing him."

Terra's eyes welled up. "I can't even imagine…" She'd only just found Kaden, and she already refused to picture her life without him.

"With any luck, that's something you'll never have to experience, my child." She smiled kindly. "When I lost my mate, all I had was this ranch and my boys and I loved them all. As well as every wolf who walked through my door. Each was a special gift and filled up the empty space a little more." She drew in a breath and scowled. "And let me tell you—this *Wolf Hunter* isn't anywhere near strong enough to take those things from me. There's no person on this planet who could make me leave this home I built with my mate."

The tears spilled from the corners of Terra's eyes, and she let them. Then she threw her arms around Mama River once again. "I swear to God—everyone is stronger than I am!"

Mama River hugged her, but then drew back and firmly held her by the shoulders. "That's nonsense! You simply feel the pain of the world more, Terra. I've watched you, my child. You carry all the emotions of the world inside you. You feel and see things that the rest of us aren't strong enough to look straight in the eye, face-to-face. You do that… and yet you still go on. That is *not* weakness, my girl. That is the very definition of strength. And now, if this man, Kaden Grant, is your mate… well, you hold onto that man just as hard and as long as you can."

Terra wiped the tears from her face and nodded jerkily. "I will."

"Then you have my support one hundred percent." She cocked her head to the side. "But your mate will be the center of your life. And part of your family, too. Do Trent and Cassie know about this?"

"Not yet." Terra cringed. Mama River was right—she'd have to call them and tell them, even though she was dreading it.

Mama River lifted Terra's chin with a single finger. "Be strong. Call them. I'll leave you be, but let me know if you need anything, yes?"

"Promise."

Mama River hugged her again and slipped out the door, giving her a smile on the way out. Before Terra lost her nerve, she parked her butt on the bed, dragged out her phone, and dialed the number for the house where her little sister was hiding.

Only it wasn't Cassie who answered, but her new surrogate mom. "Hello?" Terra didn't know what she had been thinking.

"Um... hello. I'm Terra. Cassie's sister?"

"Oh, hello, Terra!" The woman's voice was bright and sunny. "Cassie will be so disappointed she missed your call. She's in school right now."

Of course she was. Cassie's life was continuing on without her. "I should've known that. Just tell her I called, okay?"

There was a slight pause. "Is everything all right?"

"Yes. I just wanted to say hi." Terra hoped the lie

didn't show in her voice. "I'll catch up with her later." She almost asked for Trent, but it wouldn't make any sense for her brother to be there, either. He was probably at his software development company, running his business and getting on with his life as well.

"I'll have her call you as soon as she gets home."

"Thanks." Terra hung up and took a deep breath before dialing her brother at the office. He hated being interrupted at work.

"In the middle of something here, Terra," Trent said when he picked up the phone.

"Just wanted to let you know I was still alive." Terra failed to keep the sarcasm out of her voice.

"*Jesus,* Terra." Trent covered the mouthpiece of his phone and barked something at someone. When he uncovered it, he sounded like he was moving. "Okay, you're alive. Duly noted. Glad to hear it." She heard a door close. "All right, I'm in my office now. What's really going on?"

"I found a mate." She let that just hang there.

"I... what?" There was silence for a moment. "What in God's name are you talking about?"

"I'm going to take Kaden as my mate." She wanted to make sure he understood this wasn't up for a vote.

Specifically, *Trent* did not get a vote on who her mate would be. It would be just like him to assume that he did.

"*The cop?*" His voice was drenched in horror and disbelief. "What the hell is that guy doing to you?" He growled, then there was the sound of something being hit, like a fist on his desk. "What the actual fuck, Terra? The policeman has seduced you, and now you think you're going to mate with a human? What kind of head trip is this guy running? I'm calling the fucking mayor. Right now. I'm getting you out of there."

"*No!*" Terra growled into the phone. "And he's not a human, Trent."

"Wait... *what?*" The sound of him sucking in a breath came through loud and clear. "Hang on. You're saying the cop who has been watching over you is not, in fact, a human like every other fucking cop in the Seattle Police Department, but is, in fact, a wolf who you have now decided is your mate."

"Yes."

Trent held the phone away from his mouth, but Terra could still hear the cursing. After a moment, he came back. "Could you *please* keep the crazy to a minimum for a while? Just a little while, Terra. We've got this Wolf Hunter after you, I just got Cassie squared away in a new school, and I've got this deal I'm trying to close—"

"You know what?" Terra cut him off. "Just forget it. Sorry to have bothered you."

"Terra —"

She didn't hear the rest because she hung up on him. She almost threw the phone across the room, but she remembered Cassie was calling her back later, and Terra didn't want her phone out of service when that happened. She tossed her phone on the bed behind her instead.

It sunk deep into the bedspread.

Terra growled and clenched her fists. Trent was more like her father than she wanted to believe. He threw himself into his work, was always banging one girl or another, living the bachelor life. This whole hate-group thing, with his family and his sister being targeted, was just a blip in his life. An inconvenience that he'd rather not deal with.

Terra sucked in a breath and blew out her frustration. No, that wasn't fair—Trent had gotten Cassie a new place to live when she had to leave the safehouse. He'd enrolled her in school, which apparently was working out well. He wasn't completely irresponsible like their father.

And he was probably just worried about Terra.

ALISA WOODS

If she was honest, it was very much like her to run off and do something stupid. Like mate with a man she barely knew... and who was part of the Seattle Police Department. Or something similarly wild and outlandish and ill-considered.

Only this time, that's not how it was.

Kaden was her destined mate, she was sure of it. She would just have to give Trent time to figure that out, too. After all, the two of them had only met once for a few minutes. In any objective way, the whole thing with her and Kaden was going crazy fast. But that's how it was with mates, at least the true ones.

Trent had to know that, too.

Terra's phone buzzed from inside the well of comforter fluff that it had buried itself in.

She growled, convinced that it was Trent calling her back, but when she looked at the caller ID, it said *unknown caller*.

She picked it up. "Hello?"

"Terra, my dear! I hope you don't mind me calling you again." It was Julius.

"No, of course not."

"I have to admit to a certain delight whenever you take my call, my dear. I'm afraid I'm still awestruck that we have this little relationship. Purely fan worship on my part, naturally. I was very much hoping that we might be able to meet again."

She'd been so busy making love to Kaden and discovering he was a wolf and hauling him up to the mountains to talk to her cousin... she hadn't gotten any work done. "I'm sorry, I don't have anything more to show you, Julius."

"That's quite all right." The excitement in his voice was a little infectious. "I have something that might interest *you*, though. It concerns the topic we discussed previously."

She sat up straighter. "You mean the white wolves?"

"Precisely. I have some new information, and a new theory I was hoping to share with you. Would it be possible for us to meet again?"

"Yes, absolutely." She was standing now. Maybe whatever Julius had found would help Kaden understand who he was. And she knew that would be the key to them being together and becoming mates. "When would you like to meet?" she asked Julius.

"As soon as befits your schedule, my dear," he said. "But I do hope you can respect the sensitive nature of our discussion. I know it might've caused you some problems the last time with your handler. But privacy in this is of the utmost importance. When can you get away for a private meeting?"

Terra winced and hesitated. There was no way Kaden would allow her to go off by herself. And there was no way she would go without telling him. Not this time. Not ever again.

But this was too important to ignore. Julius was well-connected and wealthy... and obsessed with white wolves. Whatever he'd dug up, it had to be something special to get him all worked up. She would just have to find a way to make a meetup happen. "Give me a little time to figure that out. I'm in the middle of something I need to finish up here, anyway. Can I call you back at this number?"

"Yes. Wonderful! At your convenience, Terra. I'm delighted, and we'll make it work whenever works for you. I look forward to your call."

They said goodbye, and Terra glanced around her room. It would only take a few minutes to pack things up, then they could start heading back into the city. And then she would have to find a way to talk Kaden into letting her meet with Julius alone.

CHAPTER 12

"You've got to be fucking kidding me." Kaden couldn't believe his eyes.

Noah Wilding was showing off his skills as a witch. Crackling blue energy skittered all around his hand, front and back, as he held it up for Kaden to see. In all the times Kaden had consulted with witches in the department, he'd never seen anything like it—they always worked their spells by touch. No blue magical sparks dancing all over their skin.

This was just freaky.

"I've been practicing," Noah said with a grin. "It wasn't exactly this controlled in the beginning. And Mama River doesn't like me tearing up the house, so I keep it outside."

They were out behind the main house of the estate, off to the side of the stables. The mountain peaks loomed in the distance, and there were several cottages in back as well. But Noah had brought him to an open, grassy area where half the trees had already taken the brunt of his magic.

Noah swirled his hand around a couple of times, and the blue energy coalesced into a baseball-sized mass that floated above his palm. Then he pushed his hand straight out, toward one of the trees—the magic flew from his hand so fast, Kaden couldn't track it. He just heard the explosion, then saw the flying woodchip cloud and the black charred stump left behind.

"Holy shit." Kaden's mouth was hanging open.

Noah grinned. "There's a reason why I'm here, guarding Mama River, after everyone else hightailed it out for safer territory."

Kaden managed to shut his mouth. He peered at Noah—Terra's cousin was young like they were, probably around twenty-one or twenty-two, but Noah had a weary, worn look about him. Terra had mentioned something about him being in the Army, and Kaden already knew he'd lived through some horrific experiments the government performed on shifters.

Kaden shifted his weight from one foot to the other, awkward. "So… you're a white wolf. Or a witch. I'm really not understanding how all this works."

Noah held out one hand. "Part witch." Then the other. "Part white wolf." Then he shifted before Kaden's eyes. Noah only stayed wolf for a moment, but he was definitely a white wolf. Then he quickly shifted back to human. His clothes were left in a pile in the grass, so Kaden averted his gaze. The grass rustled as Noah got dressed.

Kaden cleared his throat. "Well, I've got the white wolf part." He wasn't keen on shifting in front of Noah. It was one thing to end up naked with Terra—he *enjoyed* that—it was another thing entirely in front of a dude. And a wolf. And apparently a witch.

"Man, you don't need to shift," Noah said, apparently reading Kaden's mind. He looked up. "Seriously. We can just talk. I was just showing off." Noah had his pants back on, so Kaden could look at him again without feeling ridiculously awkward.

"Am I supposed to be able to do *that?*" He gestured to Noah's hand where the blue energy had shot out from. "Shoot blue magical fire?" He was highly, *highly,* skeptical that was going to happen.

"I don't know what you can do, man. The government injected me with serums. I think that's what brought out my inner witch. But I'm also part wolf, so there's that. From what I understand, you're half human, right?"

Kaden nodded.

"Do you have the crazy sharp blades for claws?"

"What?" Kaden leaned back. "Um... I don't think so."

"What about the superhealing?"

Kaden rubbed the back of his neck. "Yeah." He'd always been able to heal inhumanly fast. It was his first clue that he was part shifter, even before his mother told him his father had been a wolf. But even from the beginning, he knew he was different from the other wolves. Shifters heal pretty damn fast—he'd seen a lot of bloodshed in the gangs—but not as fast as him. That was one reason why he could confront the gangs—whatever they could throw at him, short of a bullet to the head, he was pretty sure he could recover from.

And he had a good chance of surviving even that.

"The experiments may have brought out my inner witch," Noah said, "but I'm second-generation to a white wolf, at best, and I've got normal wolf DNA mixed in there, too. You and Grace... sounds like you guys are first-generation, direct descendants of a white wolf, based on what you're both saying about your fathers."

"I don't know if he was a white wolf or not," Kaden growled. "I'm not sure my mother even knew—I don't think she ever saw him in his wolf form. He was just some asshole who seduced her."

Noah nodded, lips pursed. "I've been digging into this white wolf thing. You know, *research*. Sketchy stuff. Rumors mostly. Long ago, apparently, witches and wolves weren't mortal enemies. They weren't so divided. In fact, there's a rumor that they both descended from the same kind of magical creature—some kind of shape-shifting sorcerer that was super strong in all forms of magic. There was a whole race of them with different variants—some expressed more like witches, some like wolves, some like other shifters. It's like all the magical creatures you've ever heard of rolled up into one. And the way they expressed their magic was supposedly related to the relative balance of their male and female magical energies. Like, everyone had some of each, but the ratios were all over the place. Then some kind of change happened, and over time, the witches slowly became mostly female—and the shifters were mostly male."

"That's really odd," Kaden said, "but I guess it makes a kind of sense. I've always wondered why there was such a lack of female wolves."

Noah smirked. "And why they're such a handful, right? It's like they're out of balance or something. I've got cousins and a sister that bear that out, believe me."

Kaden scowled. Terra was certainly a wild thing, to be sure, but she wasn't *unbalanced*. And that was his possible-future-mate he was talking about. "So, where does that leave me? Am I a witch or a wolf?"

"I don't know, man. Maybe your magical energy swings in the direction of wolf because you're more of the, well, that type."

"What the hell does that mean?" That sounded like an insult, but Kaden couldn't quite track it.

Noah gestured to Kaden's bunched up fists and the glare that was no doubt on his face. "I mean, you do not exactly lack in masculine qualities, Officer Grant. Fuck, man, I'm just trying to help you out here."

Kaden tried to reel in his wolf's bristling. His temper had always had a hair trigger—he'd thought it was the wolf inside, but maybe it was just *him*.

He blew out some of the stress. "Hey, look... I'm sorry. This is still all new to me. It's freaking me out, to be honest. So... what you're saying is that I'm a guy's guy, and maybe that's why my magical beast, which is really something like a witch, is expressing as a wolf."

"I honestly don't know." Noah shrugged. "It's just a theory. But I know you're something different than the other wolves out there, Kaden. And if you and Terra have something going, then this is the place for you. The Wilding family has its quirks, but the River pack is straight up cool and accepting. I work for Riverwise, and those guys were a hell of a lot more accepting than my own family... at least at first."

"Good to know." Kaden didn't really understand where he was going with any of this.

Noah lifted his chin. "But don't count us Wildings out—we're coming along. We've been broken up as a pack for so long, I think we're just wired not to trust people. It's part of our DNA now."

"Yeah, I can kind of see that in Terra." And he

worried about that—her own father had somehow dropped the ball, leaving her to fend for herself as a little girl. Which made Kaden want to go pound him to the ground… except that he was still Terra's father, and that wasn't cool. But the protective side of him wanted to make up for that sad upbringing—it was way too much like his own, and he knew all the ways that could hurt. He wanted nothing more than to shower her with all the love and safety he could give. And that meant one thing—*mating*.

He still couldn't quite wrap his head around the fact that they were going to do that. Soon, if Terra had her way. And he wasn't much inclined not to let her have her way, at least in that regard.

Noah was watching him. "Hey, Terra's as wild as they come, but she's good people. And she's my cousin. I fully expect her to kick your ass if you're not treating her right, but in case that doesn't convince you…" He focused his attention on his hand and flicked his wrist a couple of times. The blue crackling energy skittered along his skin and coalesced into his palm.

Noah held it up like he might throw it in Kaden's face.

He whipped up his hands in surrender. "Okay, okay. No need to get all witchy on me."

Noah smirked and flicked the energy away. It scorched a long burn mark along the grass.

Jesus, he was going to set the damn forest on fire.

Kaden sighed. "I'm not ever going to hurt her, Noah. She's the best thing that's ever happened to me. I've just got to sort out my own mess so I can take proper care of her."

"Now you're talking," Noah said, shaking out his hand. "But I can tell you this—I've never seen her look at a man like she looks at you. That was clear as day the moment you two walked in the door. For what that's worth. Just be worthy of her, Kaden, and you'll do fine."

Kaden sucked in a breath. It was a relief to have someone else on board with this whole idea—especially someone in Terra's family, even if it was just her cousin.

"If we do end up mated," Kaden said, "I might need a new job. I don't think the police force will take too kindly to having a shifter in its midst."

Noah went back to grinning. "We can probably work something out. Hell, with all the threats we've had from the Wolf Hunter and the hate group people, everybody's working overtime to try to keep the pack safe—both packs, River and Wilding. Like I said, they're good people. I'm sure there'd be a place for someone like you."

Kaden reached out a hand to shake Noah's. "That's a tremendous load off my mind. Thanks."

Noah shook his hand and nodded. Then he lifted his chin to gesture over Kaden's shoulder. Kaden twisted to see Terra skittering out from the house and coming toward them at a half run. Her black hair was flying behind her, and her eyes were lit up. Even with her cousin standing right next to them, Kaden still wanted to haul her off into the woods and make love to her up against a tree or some damn thing.

Good God, would that burning need for her ever slow down in the slightest?

Terra reached them, all flushed and slightly breathless. "I've got a question for you," she said to Kaden. Then she looked to her cousin. "Are you done?"

Noah had a barely restrained smirk, and Kaden had a feeling he knew exactly what was going through Kaden's mind. Or maybe it was the tightening in his pants that seemed to happen every time Terra came within reach.

"Yeah, we're done for now." Noah gave Kaden a nod. "Anytime you have questions, my friend, you know where to find me."

Noah headed off back to the main house.

"What's up, baby?" Kaden asked her.

Terra's dark eyes were on fire. "I have a way to find out more about white wolves."

CHAPTER 13

Terra didn't like the tension rolling off Kaden's body in the driver's seat next to her. They were headed to the north side of Seattle to meet Julius.

"You know, I really don't like that guy," Kaden said, giving her a sideways look.

"I know." She'd already told him about Julius having new information about white wolves. "I just want to see if he knows anything, you know, *relevant* to us." Terra was partially concerned he had somehow figured out Kaden's secret, but mostly she wanted any and all information that might help him sort things out about himself.

"Fair enough." His expression softened. "I'm glad it's not in public. And I *love* that you told me this time, instead of sneaking out."

She pretended to pout. "I'll have to think of something *else* you'll need to punish me for."

"*Jesus,* Terra," he said, subtly adjusting himself. "I'd be more than happy to do whatever you'd like… *at the safehouse.*"

She grinned and reached across the barrier to squeeze his thigh—it was so strong and muscular, and her hand was so relatively small, she could barely get a grip on it. And there were definitely other parts she'd rather wrap her hand around. She slid her hand closer to the prize, but Kaden snatched her wrist off his leg.

"Oh no, none of that." He scowled at her. "We need to have a few rules about the level of teasing permissible when I'm operating a motor vehicle."

She laughed—and she loved the dangerous smile that brought out on his face—but she knew exactly how he felt. She would be just as happy to pull over and make love to him again. The sexual tension between them was *off the charts*—like she was in a constant state of heat around him. And that endless horniness was insanely distracting.

She really shouldn't make it worse, so she pulled her hand back to her own side of the car. Besides, they were arriving at their destination.

It was like no storage facility Terra had ever seen. She double-checked the GPS coordinates Julius had given them, but this was the place. Kaden tapped in the security code at the gate, which was twelve feet high and topped with barbed wire all around. Inside the fence, the facility was all stately brick-and-stone buildings, like a gentrified part of downtown hidden away in an industrial area.

The gate rattled and slid open, allowing them entrance to the neatly paved streets where rows upon rows of high-end buildings looked like mini apartments for upscale residents. Julius told her these private storage facilities were designed for the perfect climate-controlled archival of works of art and other valuables, and he wanted to show her his private collection while they talked.

Kaden wove through the streets of the miniature city, and eventually they found the address for the storage facility/apartment that belonged to Julius. He was standing outside, dressed in trim gray pants and a casual, long-sleeved black polo. Terra felt underdressed in her t-shirt and jeans. Plus she hadn't told Julius that Kaden would be along for the ride.

A brief scowl bloomed on Julius's face as they exited the car, but he was all smiles by the time they reached him.

Julius reached a hand out to shake Kaden's. "Delightful to see you again, Officer Grant."

Kaden shook his hand, but just nodded in return.

"Has Ms. Wilding explained the delicate nature of our meeting?" The tension in Julius's shoulders held them stiff and arched up.

Terra rushed to apologize before this got any worse. "Julius, I'm sorry, but Officer Grant had to come—he *is* my security detail, after all." It felt strange to refer to Kaden that way, given he was so much more to her, but she needed to reassure Julius, or it felt like he would call the whole thing off. Besides, he didn't need to know the rest, especially the part about Kaden being a white wolf himself. "I haven't told Officer Grant the nature of our previous discussion," she lied. "And he understands that we need to talk privately."

Julius's eyes brightened. "Excellent. I greatly appreciate that you've respected my privacy, Terra. I do hope you understand, Officer Grant. This way, please." Julius gestured to the stately wood-carved door that served as an entrance to his storage facility. They all took the three steps up to the landing, then Julius tapped in the security code.

The door opened to a foyer that was more *palatial estate* than *storage facility,* between the granite floors and the chandelier hanging above them, sparkling with crystal. A decorative plant was tucked in a corner, but the foyer was otherwise empty. It opened to a long hallway lined with doors—four on each side.

"If you don't mind, Officer Grant," Julius said, "you could wait here while I take Terra back to the far room, unit number four. That's where my private art collection is housed, and it will be a sufficiently private location for our little discussion as well." He gave Terra a wink.

Kaden's eyes narrowed. "How about I escort you to the door? I can wait just outside."

Julius held his hands out with what looked like a forced smile. "Of course." He led Terra and Kaden down the hall to the last door at the end, then keyed in the unlock code. The door clicked but remained closed. "If you wouldn't mind?" Julius waved Kaden back a step or two.

Terra cringed. Apparently, Julius was ridiculously possessive of his collection and didn't want Kaden to see any part of it, not even a glimpse through the open door. Kaden scowled but stepped back one deliberate pace, just enough that Julius might be able to slip in without Kaden seeing inside.

Julius's smile grew, then he turned to Terra. "Close your eyes, my dear." His eyes lit up. "I want to surprise you with the full effect once you're inside."

Terra frowned a little and threw a glance to Kaden, whose scowl was growing darker by the second.

"Oh, please do indulge me in this small drama!" Julius said with a pleading smile. "This is a little fantasy of mine, sharing my collection with you. But if it makes you uncomfortable, my dear…"

Terra shook her head. "No, no. It's fine." She closed her eyes and reached out with her hands. "Lead the way."

Julius grasped one of her hands. "You won't be disappointed, my dear." He gently tugged her forward. She kept one hand along the wall to feel her way. He pulled the door open and then ushered her through.

"Keep them closed now!" Julius chastised lightly. "Until I tell you to open up."

She heard the door click closed behind her, and she

dutifully kept her eyes closed, but she could sense the change in pressure and temperature and humidity inside the room. It was definitely a climate-controlled facility. The anticipation in her grew as Julius scuffed around behind her for a moment.

"Just one second while I find the lights," he said, and then he was behind her, his hands resting gently on her shoulders. "Now! Open your eyes, Terra."

She blinked them open, and it took her second to focus.

What she saw didn't make any sense.

The room was large—two stories tall—and its walls were plastered with photographs and papers and screens and what looked like string tying them all together. The string connected one image to another. Some radiated out from a central photograph. As she peered closer, she saw one photograph was hers—the wolf pup from the shifter gang that she gave Julius. She glanced at the screens, which were playing videos... *the Wolf Hunter's videos.*

"What is this?" she asked, horrified.

"This is *you*," Julius whispered in her ear, his hands gripping harder on her shoulders.

He was surprisingly strong.

Panic zoomed through her system—but before she could shift out of his grasp, he grabbed the back of her neck, and something sharp pinched her.

He had injected her with something.

The room swam in front of her eyes, and her knees buckled.

Julius caught her under the arms and kept her from hitting the floor.

"Do you like my collection, Terra?" He turned her toward the nearest wall, but she was so woozy, she could barely focus. When she did, she saw the entire wall was covered with pictures of *her.* "I made it especially for you," he said in her ear.

Her stomach heaved. She opened her mouth to scream, but Julius's hand was over it, suffocating her. She tried to shift again, but her wolf was gone... *absent...* banished deep into her mind.

The room started to dim around her.

Julius dragged her limp form across the floor. The last thing she saw was the Wolf Hunter video restarting.

It was the one where he had dismembered a wolf.

When Terra came to, she was in a completely different place. Her stomach was still heaving from whatever Julius had injected her with, and her body felt like it had been completely drained of energy. She blearily opened her eyes.

She was in a small room, sitting in a chair, with Julius standing in front of her. When she tried to move, it was clear her arms and legs were tied to the chair. Her first instinct was to shift out of the restraints, but she couldn't. Just like before, her wolf was simply... *gone*.

A shiver ran through her.

"No, you won't be able to shift," Julius said with a smirk. His arms were crossed, and he was leaning against a closed door. "At least not for a while. The drug will see to that. A little gift, courtesy of my dearly departed friend—the one you called Agent Smith. I figured it would make the interrogation a little easier if I weren't chasing you all over the room."

God, what was happening? "Why are you doing this?"

"I thought that would be obvious by now," Julius sneered. "I guess the brainy part of the gene pool didn't land on your side." All the gentility was gone.

A cold shudder shook her body, ending in an icy trickle that landed in her stomach. *She was alone in this.* Kaden may not even know she was gone... he certainly wouldn't know where to find her. Her mate wasn't going to save her.

Death had finally caught up with her, after all.

"What do you want to know?" she spat at Julius. He mentioned something about interrogation; there had to be *something* he was after.

"I want to know who the white wolf is." Julius said this like it was completely obvious what he was talking about, not some vague nonsense. He opened his mouth to say more, but he was interrupted by a knock at the door behind him.

He scowled and turned to open it. A rough-looking man in black tactical gear stood outside the doorway. He toted a massive gun, plus he had several more weapons strapped to his sides.

"Sir, the mayor is on the line," the man said.

"I'll call him back," Julius said sharply. "Don't interrupt me again unless we're actually being assaulted."

The man ducked his head and quickly closed the door.

Julius trained his hungry gaze on her again.

Oh God. What was he going to do to her?

"Nothing's going to distract us now, Terra. I almost didn't think we'd get here today… your handler from the Seattle Police Department was unusually competent at his job. Which could end up being very unfortunate… for him."

"Leave Kaden alone!" The words just gushed out of her, but she wished she hadn't said anything, not with the way Julius's eyebrows lifted.

"Is that right? I see... you've been banging the security guard. *Typical.* Little sexy wolf vixen seducing every human that comes along her path." He sauntered closer to her.

She leaned back in her chair to get away from him, but she had nowhere to go. Her face wrinkled up in disgust, but she didn't say anything more—Julius still thought Kaden was a human, and it was better for him if it stayed that way.

But she prayed he would come for her. He was her mate, or at least he was supposed to be. But her fuzzed-out brain couldn't imagine how he could find her.

She'd been so foolish.

"But let's get right to the point, shall we?" Julius said. "How about you simply tell me the truth—who is the white wolf?"

"I don't know what you're talking about!" And that was mostly true. Julius couldn't know about Kaden being a white wolf—was he talking about Noah? She didn't think anyone knew about that, either, at least outside of the packs. Julius was chasing some kind of rumor or ghost about this mythical white wolf he was obsessed with...

Except now she knew who Julius was—*the Wolf Hunter*. Or at least, one of the Wolf Hunter's followers. Julius had practically made a shrine to the Wolf Hunter in that crazy-obsessive room filled with her pictures and pictures of her family.

"Come on, Terra," Julius said, his voice rising in anger. "You're not that stupid."

She frowned, but she was genuinely confused. "You want the white wolf, but I don't even know what that is. I was coming to *you* to find out!"

He drew back and frowned at her. "You were rather eager to come by and find out more about the white wolf, weren't you? But then again that's part of your family lore, isn't it? Or should I say, the family *shame?*"

He was talking about her grandfather's brother—the white wolf that broke up the Wilding pack.

"What do you know about that?" she asked, eyes wide. If he knew that, what else did he know?

"As you saw from my wall, I know quite a bit about you and your family," he sneered. "I kept thinking that the white wolf would come to the rescue of his darling children and grandchildren as I blew them up one by one... *but no.* Apparently, he's just as much of a bastard as I expected. So in the absence of some kind of flushing out, as was my original intention, I'm having to resort to *this.*" He gestured to her, tied up in the chair.

"You think I know where my grandfather's brother is?" she asked like he was crazy. Because he clearly was. "He broke up the family two generations ago. We haven't seen him since."

Julius rushed forward and braced his hands on the chair arms on either side of her. She jerked in her chair with surprise, but there wasn't anywhere she could go with her hands and legs firmly tied down.

Julius's face was far too close to hers. "Yes, do tell me about how he broke up your family." She could feel his hot breath on her face. "Permit me a little *schadenfreude* at the Wilding family's dysfunctional mess. But what can you expect from a man—or should I say *wolf*—who broke the basic covenant of the pack by sleeping with his alpha's mate? It's a beautiful irony, I must admit." He eased back from her, looking amused again. "Tell me what you know, Terra Wilding, and I'll consider letting you live."

She gave him another look like he was crazy, but she

couldn't see any reason not to tell him something that he clearly already knew. She just couldn't say anything about Noah or Kaden or any of her family who were alive now. "You seem to know the story already. My grandfather's brother slept with his mate. It broke up the pack. As far as I'm concerned, that's all in the past."

Julius's eyes narrowed. "But it's not all in the past, is it? There are more white wolves, alive today... not least, the determined Grace Krepky. She was the one who, shall we say, awakened my understanding of the situation."

Terra drew back again. "I don't understand."

Julius's dark blue eyes lit up. "It's really quite simple when you connect all the dots. There's a white wolf roaming our city. He's extremely powerful. And he likes to fuck around with human women. It's possible that he's not simply a wolf, but also a witch—which only means that his powers are even more extensive. And he's been sleeping with them for a long time. Decades to be precise."

Terra pressed her lips tight—she wasn't saying anything more, nothing that might lead him to Kaden.

"Grace was my first clue that he was still around," Julius said. "You see, she's rather young. Much younger than my thirty-two years, which means that the white wolf was still fucking around Seattle as recently as twenty years ago. The only question is—is he still here, and if so, where?"

Terra frowned. What did he mean, younger than his thirty-two years? "Are you saying… wait, you knew about the white wolf *before* Grace came out?" Was he saying what she thought?

"Maybe you're not so stupid after all," Julius sniffed. "Yes, I was aware of the white wolf's antics before our representative-hopeful came on the scene." He stepped back…

…and then he shifted. *Into a white wolf.*

"Holy shit." Terra's mouth hung open.

Julius shifted human again, suddenly standing before her, completely naked. His trim, tailored clothes were lying in a heap on the floor. She didn't miss the way his erection was slowly growing… and it made her throat suddenly run dry.

Julius sauntered over to her, not hiding his nakedness at all. In fact, he seemed to want to flaunt it in her face. He leaned his hands on the chair again, coming sickeningly close. "Holy shit, indeed." His voice was a restrained laugh.

She leaned away, disgusted, and prayed he didn't plan to do anything repulsive with that body of his. Like touch her with it.

"I'm not interested in fucking you, Terra, if that's what you're thinking." His words were belied by his oily and lecherous voice. "Although maybe there'll be time for that before were done. What I want is something much more exciting—revenge."

"Revenge on who?" She couldn't keep the disgust out of her voice… or the fear.

"On my father."

His father? Maybe his father was actually her grandfather. Maybe he was Kaden's father. Either way, it didn't matter. Because she didn't have any answers for Julius.

And, because of that, she was sure that this time… death would finally catch up to her.

CHAPTER 14

Kaden was tired of waiting.

Terra and that asshole, Julius, and been in his little collection room for way too damn long.

Kaden pounded on the door. Waited. Pounded again. Nothing.

Fuck this.

He dug out his cell phone and called Terra's. It rang and rang... and then went to message. He pounded on the door again. It was possible the cell phone reception wasn't getting through the thick stone walls of this place, but there was no way the room was so locked-tight soundproof that they couldn't hear him pounding.

They were ignoring him.

Whatever juicy information Terra was getting about white wolves, he didn't give a damn.

Their time was up.

He searched for the number of the manager of the facility and dialed.

When someone picked up he used his most *I'm a cop, don't fuck with me* voice. "This is Officer Grant from the Seattle Police Department. I've got reasonable cause a crime is being committed on your premises. I need access to Unit Ninety Three. *Immediately.*"

"I… um…" The woman's voice on the other end was high and panicked. *Good.* "I'll be right there, Officer!"

She hung up.

Kaden timed it, and she it only took two minutes to get there, but he was going out of his fucking mind in the meantime. He even shifted his hand and tried to slice his way through the door, but he didn't have whatever badass claws Noah was talking about, and underneath the stately carved wood, the door was solid steel. At least an inch thick, maybe two. He was getting nowhere, but he still clawed the shit out of it. He was tempted to rip into the control pad, but he might jam it up, and that would just make things worse.

A short, hunch-shouldered woman scurried in through the storage facility door, her little sensible shoes making no noise on the granite flooring.

"Oh!" she said when she arrived at his side and looked at the door with a wide-eyed stare. "What happened?"

"Open the door, Ma'am," he ordered, his voice full of growl.

She almost jumped out of her skin, then scrambled to tap out the override code. The door clicked open. Kaden shoved her side as gently as he could manage and barreled into the room with his weapon drawn.

It was empty.

At least, the room was empty of *people*—there was a whole fucking rats-nest of crazy, though. Pictures of people and wolves filled every inch of the wall. Videos played on large screens. He only had to take one look at those to recognize them.

The Wolf Hunter.

"Fuck!" He couldn't believe it. Fucking Julius was the Wolf Hunter—or at least as bat-shit crazy as that maniac—and now he had Terra.

Kaden whirled on the mousy manager, who was quivering by the door. "Is there another way out?" There had to be. He'd been watching the door the entire time. They sure as hell didn't leave the way they came in.

The woman nodded frantically and pointed a shaky finger toward the far end of the room. Kaden sprinted over and found a door in the wall, nearly hidden by all the photos plastered on and around it.

"Open this up!" he shouted.

She did, but there was nothing to see—just another hallway, and at the end of that, a door that led outside. Once Kaden spilled out into the sunshine, he realized... they could be anywhere. They had at least a twenty-minute head start before he started banging on the door.

Shit.

A cold darkness clamped down on his chest, the same feeling of panic when he found her missing the first time. *He'd lost her.* For a long, scattered moment, his brain clouded with fury and terror.

Then he pulled his shit together.

That asshole had taken his mate, and he was going to get her back.

He sprinted back to his car, shutting down his emotions—he could deal with those later—and trying to engage his brain to figure out what do to next.

He couldn't go to the department—they would just laugh. And probably reassign him to another case. They sure as hell weren't going to help him.

But Noah Wilding might.

Kaden climbed in his car and threw it into gear, heading for the front gate. He dialed Noah's number as he went.

Noah picked up on the first ring. "Hello?"

"The Wolf Hunter has taken Terra," Kaden said, no time to waste.

"Fuck." But Noah recovered quickly. "Where are you? How can I help?"

Kaden had a sudden, huge appreciation for the fact that Noah was Army trained and packed some badass magical energy. "Are you still at the River estate?" Kaden needed to *move,* and he was just now realizing that, while he could really use Noah's help, he couldn't afford to wait.

"Yeah, are you in the city?"

"I'm on the north side, but I have no idea where he's taken Terra. Just get your ass down off the mountain, and I'll call back with directions as soon as I know."

"Copy that." Noah hung up.

Kaden tossed his phone into the passenger seat next to him. Then he growled and pounded on the steering wheel. Venting some of the frustration would help him think.

Noah was too far.

The department was useless.

What did that leave him?

Whenever the department needed to find someone— usually a shifter, but other criminals too—they brought in the witches. And the ones he worked with had an office downtown.

Witches were crazy dangerous to work with, but he didn't care. He needed a seeking spell, and they were the only ones who could find Terra before it was too late. He couldn't let his mind go there, so he just floored it. He ran a few red lights on the way, but he got there in record time.

This coven of witches—there were several in the city—ran a boutique ad agency focused on online services. Their shiny glass-and-chrome office was on the 14th floor. Kaden illegally parked in the underground parking garage next to the elevator. He was tempted to simply *run* up the stairs, but fourteen floors would take too damn long. The elevator was faster, but he was chomping at the bit the entire way. When he spilled out of it, he charged inside their high-end office, ignoring the receptionist and stomping his way through the cubicle-land of witches to get to the one he knew—*Xena Hunt*.

He had no idea if that was her real name. He didn't care.

He flung open her door without knocking, and thankfully, she was there.

Xena was voluptuous and beautiful, the way all the witches were. They used some kind of magic spell to enhance their beauty, and he was always knocked out by their supermodel bodies and drop-dead sexy faces. But this time, none of that affected him. He rushed straight up to her desk, planted his hands, and demanded that she tear her attention away from her fucking computer.

"Xena," he growled when she ignored him. "I need your help."

She finally deigned to look at him, but only to lean back and scrunch up her pretty little nose. "Is this how you ask for favors, Officer Grant? I'd hate to see what you do when you're demanding something." Her sexy half-smirk said she expected the possibility of him making demands on her to be approximately zero.

"Please." He didn't have time to fuck around.

She looked unimpressed, but she did rise up from her chair and saunter around the desk. The long look she gave him, starting at his crotch working up to his eyes, couldn't have been any more obvious. The witches flirted with him all the time, but he'd never been stupid enough to take one to bed. These women killed people with a single touch—and interrogated wolves with some pretty fucked up and painful spells.

Her lips formed a beautiful little pout. "How exactly can the Seattle Police Department use my help today?" Her voice was all sultry and sexy.

"I need to find someone. She's a shifter, and she was in my custody, but now she's been kidnapped." Just saying those words out loud was making his blood boil. His fists clenched at his side.

She *tsk-tsked* him and then brushed her cascading waves of warm, brown hair behind her shoulder. "You've lost one of your toys? How unfortunate. But I don't see how that's any of my concern." She raked her gaze over him again. "Unless, of course, there's something in it for me."

He couldn't promise the normal payout, and here she was asking for some kind of bribe on top. *Shit.* "What do you want, Xena? This is a *kidnapping.* I've got a ticking clock."

She raised her eyebrows. "You want a favor and you're in a hurry. Sounds to me like unusual circumstances that might require unusual forms of payment."

She eased closer to him, close enough that she could reach out and touch him, but she didn't. Probably because his body was taut with anger, fear, and a huge helping of revulsion.

He leaned away. "I can make sure the department funnels all their cases through you for the next month or two," he offered. "I'll see what other business we can throw your way. And I'll make sure you're not burdened with an unexpected regulatory investigation."

Her green eyes flashed, and he was afraid he might have pushed it too far with the threat. But she just wagged a finger at him. "Now, now, Officer Grant, there's no need for that." She closed the gap between them and landed her hand directly on his cock. "Besides, you know what I want."

Jesus Christ. He grabbed hold of her wrist and hauled it up to face level. "I don't have time to fuck around, Xena."

Her green eyes blazed again—it was flat dangerous to

touch a witch, but it seemed to be turning her on. Which was not exactly his intent. *Shit.*

"Well, of course, we'll find your little toy first," she purred, easing her body into his with her perfectly perky breasts pressing against his chest. "Payment after services rendered, of course."

Fine. He would promise whatever the witch wanted, then hope she wouldn't actually kill him when he failed to deliver. "Do the seeking spell, Xena. We can party all you like later." He had no intention of following through, but the words were still chalky in his mouth. Terra was the only woman he ever wanted to touch that way, but he would do whatever was necessary to get his mate back alive.

"Excellent." Xena sauntered away from him to one of the bookshelves in her office—they held a wide range of strange pots and exotic boxes. Kaden didn't even want to know what was inside.

The witch opened one and pulled out a pinch of white powder, sifting it down into the palm of her hand. Then she said some kind of incantation as she waved her hand over the powder. It stirred with an unseen wind—a magical wind—and a whitish cloud formed above it. Blue sparks zipped around in the cloud, eerily familiar. It was the same sort of magical energy Noah had showed him.

Xena swayed her hips as she walked back toward him. "Do you have a good memory of this toy you wish to find?"

He'd done seeking spells with her before—he knew the routine—but usually, the spell was done on someone else. Someone who had a personal connection to the suspect they were seeking. Only this time, *he* was the one who had the connection. A *very* personal connection.

He gritted his teeth. "I do."

She stepped up to him and blew the small cloud into his face.

He was ready for it, but the way the ground shifted under his feet still caught him by surprise. The room went blurry, and suddenly he was mentally back in the safehouse, on the bed with Terra, sinking his cock deep inside her. She was moaning and writhing underneath him.

Xena's voice boomed into the vision, suddenly loud and like she was calling to him from down a long tunnel. *"Oh my.* I see we've been playing with our toys."

Kaden felt sick to his stomach—he hated violating that memory by sharing it with the witch, but he knew she needed some kind of access to Terra's magical signature to find her. Thankfully, the vision quickly ended. He was still unsteady, but the effects of the spell quickly dissipated once Xena had found what she wanted.

Kaden rubbed his eyes with both hands to get them clear. "Did you find her?" he demanded.

"Oh, yes. She is strong in magic." Xena's eyes narrowed. "But then again, so are you, Kaden Grant... why didn't you tell me you were a witch?"

Oh, shit. "That's not exactly public knowledge," he said tightly.

Her smile smoldered. "Oh, how I'd love to use that knowledge to blackmail you into some hot, hot sex like I saw in your vision." She sighed with a kind of lusty disappointment and fanned herself with long fingers tipped with even longer nails. "But your magic's just a little too powerful for me to handle. Plus there's that pesky bond you have with the girl." She fluttered her fingers at the space around his head—he was pretty sure she was talking about his aura. Witches could see your emotions on display like a fucking rainbow around your head. Generally useful, but annoying at the moment. "I'd hate to get caught in that little vortex." She looked him up and down again. "It's a damn shame, though. I was really looking forward to—"

"*Xena,*" he warned, although he was relieved to be off the hook for taking her to bed. "Do you know where Terra is or not?"

"Yes, of course." She scowled at him, like he had somehow doubted her magical ability. "I can give you the coordinates, precisely. But Kaden…" She eased a little closer, but this time, the concern on her face seemed to be genuine. "There's a lot of magical energy where you're headed. Negative energy. And I sense that you… you haven't really come into your powers yet. Be careful."

Kaden's eyebrows flew up, and he was at a loss for words for a moment. Then he said, "Thanks for the warning."

She tipped her head to him. "We witches have to look out for one another. Let me know when you're ready to explore your magic, hot stuff."

He wasn't *at all* sure he'd wanted to take her up on that offer, but none of that mattered to him right now. He got the coordinates for Terra's location and hurried out of the office, leaving a wave of turning heads behind him. He hadn't even reached the elevator again before he was dialing his phone.

Noah picked up right away. "I know where she is," Kaden said. "And I'm sending you directions. Meet you there."

He punched the elevator button and growled his impatience all the way down.

CHAPTER 15

Julius was still hovering over Terra, his naked body sickeningly close to hers.

She shuddered as his erection brushed against her leg.

He was clearly crazy and messed up—she had to talk her way out of this or she was going to end up dead, sooner rather than later. And she still was holding out hope that Kaden might come for her, but who knew how long that would take?

"Why do you want revenge on your father?" Terra

asked Julius as calmly as she could while he was raking his gaze over her body. She genuinely didn't understand this thing with the father. She was still reeling from the fact that he was a white wolf, but why would that piss him off at his father? She was still trying to pick through the pieces, the lies and half-lies, to figure out the full truth of what was going on here.

Julius ignored her question, obviously enjoying her discomfort with his erection sliding against her leg. *So disgusting.* At least her jeans kept the contact to a minimum. He captured a stray lock of her hair in one hand and wound it around his finger.

"You wolves really are incredibly seductive, aren't you?" He grabbed a bigger chunk of her hair and pulled it painfully. He was stronger than he looked, and that hold forced her head back so she had to look up at him. He licked his lips. "Your insatiable sexual appetites are running ravage through our city. My father was just like you, seducing humans all over Seattle. Including my mother. Only he didn't stick around to watch her die from the demon seed he planted in her."

Terra frowned and tried to pull out of his hold, but he just tightened his grip. She still couldn't shift to get away—whatever drug he had given her was suppressing her wolf—and being tied to the chair, she was pretty much at his mercy. And his lean form was deceptively strong; he definitely had shifter strength, even as a halfling.

But the thing that freaked her out most was his story. It was so like Kaden's. A white wolf sleeping with his human mother and leaving before the resulting halfling was born? Were they half-brothers? Was this white wolf really still roaming the city?

"So your mother is dead?" Terra swallowed down her nerves and tried to keep her voice steady. "I know what that's like." She was making a play for common ground, even though it was turning her stomach. Her empathetic response Julius's hate-filled rant just might buy her some time.

She had to get out of this somehow. Kaden needed her.

It worked a little. Julius released her hair and eased back, no longer touching her with his naked body parts. She repressed the sigh of relief.

"My mother died in childbirth... giving birth to a monstrosity. *Me.*" Julius gestured to his naked body. "This human form is just a deception. It covers up the wolf that lingers inside me, the part left over from the monster who sired me. I can't change the wolf inside me—believe me, I've tried." He gave a small, mirthless laugh. "But I can make my father pay for what he did."

"If your mother died in childbirth…" Terra's mind was grasping at something that didn't quite make sense. "How do you know *she* wasn't a wolf?"

Julius surged forward and smacked the arms of her chair on either side, making her jerk in response. "Because I know!" He heaved hot breath in her face and clamped her chin his hand. He held her tight and stared into her eyes. "I didn't grow up a pampered princess, like you, Ms. Wilding. I grew up in Seattle's foster system, tossed from home to home. I never knew my birth mother, but I know she died of severe complications in childbirth… *because I shifted when I was still in the womb.* A human woman is not meant to carry a beast. My father did that to her."

Holy shit. He killed his mother. At birth. That was so… messed up. And Terra didn't understand it at all— human women carried halflings to term all the time. Something must have gone wrong… and Julius thought it was his beast that did it.

She held perfectly still, unprepared to deal with that level of crazy.

Julius's heaving breath calmed a little. He shoved her head aside as he eased back, seeming more in control now. "I didn't know all of this at first, of course. I didn't shift again until I was much older. But when I did, I knew there was something different about me. As you've seen, I'm no common wolf." He smirked. "And when Grace Krepky revealed herself to be a white wolf as well—well, then the hunt was *on*."

Terra's heart was pounding, but she kept still and quiet and let him rant.

"I used every resource I had to open up my birth records. I wanted to know what had *really* happened to my mother. It took several bribes and not a few threats to discover the truth. Along the way, I stumbled upon the fact that the Wilding family was *also* descended from a white wolf." He stepped back and spread his arms wide, still naked, but his erection had finally fallen.

That gave Terra only a small bit of comfort.

Julius tipped his head back to look up at the ceiling. "The entire city of Seattle needs to be purged of this wolf scourge!" Then he snapped his blue eyes back to her. "But so far, my attempts to do so have not flushed my father out from whatever rock he is hiding under. Now *you*, Terra Wilding… you're going to tell me what I want to know. Where is the white wolf?"

"I don't know anything!" She put as much truth into her voice as she could.

He narrowed his eyes. Then he eased forward again, this time running his hand over her body, cupping her breasts and kneeling down to brush his body against her. She shuddered and turned her face away.

"If that's so, then I'll have to find an unfortunate end for you. But before that happens, maybe I'll enjoy a little taste of Wilding for myself."

She braced herself. He would have to untie her to really assault her. Maybe. But if he let her loose, whether she could shift or not, she would scratch the living hell out of him and fight him every step of the way. Her body trembled as his touch grew more urgent. Her stomach heaved as he reached down to stroke himself, bringing his erection back.

God no. No, no, no—

A pounding at the door made them both start.

"I told you no interruptions!" Julius roared.

Several sharp pops resounded from outside the door. It opened, and the tactical-gear guy from before poked his head in. He ran a quick scan over Julius's naked body but seemed unfazed.

Or maybe he was just freaked about the gunfire outside—at least it sounded like gunfire.

He had to shout over the shots. "Someone kicked down the front door. We've got two unfriendlies and a lot of firepower."

Terra's heart raced—*Kaden was here!*

"Hold them off," Julius growled while grabbing for his pants. "And send James and Richard back here."

"Yes, sir." The man ducked back out, closing the door behind him.

Terra squirmed in her chair, but she was held tight by her bindings. She wanted to scream out, but she wasn't sure if Kaden was close enough to hear her... and she'd probably only get one chance with that.

Julius was swearing as he shoved on his clothes. Then he pulled a knife from his pocket, unfolded it, and lunged for her. She shrieked.

"Shut up." He locked her head under his arm and muffled her mouth against his leg. She was seriously tempted to bite him... but he was cutting her bindings loose.

He was moving her.

And that would be her chance.

As soon as she was free, she bolted out of the chair

and for the door.

"Oh no, you don't." Julius was right behind her, grabbing her around the throat just as she wrenched open the door. She fought against his hold, but he was too strong for her. He was a shifter, after all, if not an obviously muscular one. That was how she missed it in the beginning.

With the door open, the sporadic gunfire was insanely loud. The popping sounds ricocheted around the cavernous warehouse outside the door. Tall shelving and pallets of goods spread across the concrete floor and blocked a lot of her view, but there was definitely some kind of fight going on at the far end. Several tactical-gear-clad men had taken cover behind the pallets, but they were aiming at the open door that must lead to the front of the building. Two other figures hid just outside the doorway, their guns making brief appearances to volley shots back.

"Kaden!" Terra screamed, and her voice bounced across the hard surfaces of the warehouse. She thought she heard a growl in response, but then Julius's hand was over her mouth, cutting off any second chance to scream. He hauled her, kicking and fighting, across the floor, further from the gunfight. She grabbed hold of a pallet as they passed, getting a strong enough grip to stop him.

Suddenly, something cold and hard pressed into her side. "I've no qualms about killing you," Julius hissed. "I'd much rather leaving you bleeding out on the concrete than give you over to whatever pack is trying to rescue you."

She believed him.

She stopped fighting.

Two of Julius's men joined them, forming a tight brigade as he hauled her toward the back door, one hand on her throat, the other holding a gun to her side. Outside, the sun had sunk below the horizon, and the alley was growing dark. The gunfire behind them stepped up a notch, battering her eardrums. She prayed none of the bullets would find Kaden. She wasn't even sure it was him—there were two gunmen, and she hadn't seen either one clearly—but it simply *had* to be. He was her mate. He had come for her.

Even if death found her via Julius's gun pressed to her side, at least she would die knowing Kaden loved her. They hadn't had a chance to say the words, but his actions said everything.

She stumbled as Julius dragged her across the alleyway that backed up to the warehouse. They were in some kind of industrial district, and there was a shiny black sedan parked in the limited spaces along the red-bricked buildings.

A crackle of electrical energy and an explosion sounded behind them. Something had changed in the fight in the warehouse. Shouts and stomping of feet said someone was coming.

"Move, move!" one of Julius's men shouted. He and the other one hustled her and Julius toward an oversized metallic dumpster on the way to the sedan. Just as they reached it, the door to the warehouse slammed open.

"Terra!" Kaden's voice roared across the alleyway.

She twisted to just barely glimpse him in the murk inside the doorway. "Kaden—" Her scream was cut off by Julius's hand muffling her mouth again. He tucked behind the dumpster along with his men, shoving her body out where Kaden could see.

"You want her?" Julius shouted hoarsely. "Come and get her!"

No! It was a trap! She shook her head violently against Julius's hold, but it was no use—he had too hard a grip on her—but she could see his men creeping around the back of the dumpster, ready to shoot Kaden as soon as he emerged from the cover of the doorway.

She bit hard on Julius's hand.

"Fuck!" He wrenched his hand off her mouth.

"Kaden, no!" she managed to get out before Julius punched her stone-cold to the side of her face. It knocked her down to the ground. Julius had her by the hair in an instant, hauling her back up, but a deafening roar filled her ears.

Kaden sprang out of the doorway, shifting mid-air in his leap.

"No!" she screamed.

A hail of bullets pounded into his body mid-flight, punching holes into the man she loved. She watched in horror as he fell, bouncing hard on the pavement. Then he struggled to his feet, dragging himself toward dumpster as more bullets wracked his snow-white body, blossoming it with red. Her heart wrenched like she was dying. She turned on Julius, screaming and kicking and clawing at his face. He raised his gun to point at her head—

Suddenly the dumpster heaved sideways, crashing into Julius and knocking him off his feet. Blue magical energy skittered along the surface and dissipated into the air. Terra stared open-mouthed at Kaden's raised paw, where the bolt had come from. Then he slumped to the ground just as Noah appeared in the doorway. Noah ducked back for cover. She could see another blue ball forming in the dark.

Behind her, Julius was scrambling away on all fours. One of his men was down, flat on his back on the alley floor, his gun fallen by his side, but the other had pried up a manhole cover a short distance away. Julius slipped down the hole as another blast of blue energy—this one from Noah—took out his minion, throwing him back against the brick wall of the alley and leaving him charred and slumped on the ground.

Something soft nuzzled her arm, and Terra turned to find Kaden had dragged himself across the alley to her.

"Oh, God!" The air rushed out of her as she wrapped her arms around his wolf. He collapsed next to her, his furry head butting up against her face. His beautiful white coat was drenched with red—blood, so much blood, and so many wounds. Tears blurred her eyes as she stroked him, comforted him. But her heart was frozen with fear. *He was dying in her arms.*

Noah hurried up to her side, another blue fireball floating above his hand. "Where did he go?" he demanded. He meant Julius.

Terra motioned toward the manhole with her head;

she couldn't even see through the tears. "Down the hole," she managed to gasp out, her attention still on her mate.

Noah sprinted over to the hole and blasted his magical energy down it, calling, "Take that, fucker!" He peered after it, looking for something.

But Terra didn't care. Julius didn't matter. Only Kaden in her arms did.

"You can't die," she sobbed, cradling his face.

His dark blue eyes focused on her, blinking long and slow. She knew it was bad—otherwise, he would have shifted by now. He must have lost too much blood to have the magic left to make it happen.

"Don't you understand?" Her tears were falling on the red-flecked fur of his face. "I'm the one who's supposed to die, not you." She kissed his face, again and again, whispering her love to him. Saying the words that only he would hear, before it was too late. So he would *know*, just as she did.

Noah was back, kneeling at Kaden's side. "Come on, you asshole. This is no place to die." But he was looking over Kaden's body with concern.

Terra ignored him, just nuzzled Kaden's face to hers. He was squirming in her arms, the pain obviously wracking his body as the life ebbed from it. Her sobs were the only sound in the alleyway... until a small plinking sound repeated itself, once, twice, three times...

She finally looked up from her hug—and then stared in amazement at Kaden's body.

"No fucking way," Noah breathed.

The bullets that riddled Kaden's pelt were, one by one, working their way out of his flesh and falling to the pavement, plinking and rolling a short distance away.

"What... what is happening?" she asked Noah, breath frozen in her chest.

"This badass mate of yours is healing himself." There was a small laugh of surprise and awe in Noah's voice.

But it was true.

As she watched, Kaden's body expelled bullet after bullet. His squirming wasn't a death-throe... it was his body healing itself of gunshot wounds.

A spattering of footsteps made her heart seize up... but it was just the police, a dozen of them, spilling out of the doorway of the warehouse with their guns drawn. Someone was shouting orders, but they mostly stopped and stared at her and Noah crouched next to Kaden in his blazing-white wolf form, drenched in blood, bullets spitting one-by-one out of his body.

After a long, tense moment, Kaden shifted in her arms, ending up naked and human on the alleyway pavement next to her. The bullets scattered away under his movement to take her in his arms and hold her.

"Are you all right?" he asked.

A crazy, joyful laugh bubbled up from deep inside her. She held hard onto him. "You're the one who's been shot."

Kaden pulled back and ran his gaze over her. "Are you sure he didn't hurt you? Please tell me you're really okay."

She cupped his cheeks in her hands. "I'm far better than okay," she said, tears still streaming from the corners of her eyes. "I have you."

Then he kissed her as if it didn't matter that the whole world was watching.

Because it didn't.

CHAPTER 16

"You're kidding me, right?" Kaden couldn't believe Terra was insisting on shooting pictures of him before they got down to the serious business of the day, which was the same business he should have every day—claiming her for his mate.

Of course, that was *his* agenda—he wasn't planning on leaving this little cottage on the back lot of the River family's estate without sinking his teeth into her. He'd gotten all the information he needed from Noah about the particulars of the mating ritual. Terra had already submitted to him—all he needed was for her to settle down and stop hopping around him with that camera glued to her face. Then he'd make her scream his name and take her the way only an alpha could take his mate.

She didn't know any of this... but it was his intention all the same.

"Shut up and be gorgeous," she said, moving around him and snapping her camera. Then she focused in on his tattoo. The words *Protect* and *Serve* had been marred a little by the bullets that had sprayed his body in the alleyway. It had been less than a day, and his body might have insane healing powers, but he was still pockmarked by the scars. Probably would be for life.

Terra seemed to find them fascinating.

It was turning her on, photographing him nude with all his battle wounds now healed. And her pictures were getting an eyeful of his cock as well, given it was turning him on, too. Which was all to the good, if she would just put the camera away.

"These are private use only, right?" he asked, as he watched her flit around him. "I don't have to worry about these showing up on the internet, do I?"

She grinned behind her camera, then looked up to

intentionally lick her lips. "I'll save the best ones for when you're on duty, and I need something to feed my fantasies."

He growled. The idea of her getting off on pictures of him twisted him around something fierce. "Okay, that's enough." He reached out and took her camera, ignoring her pout when he did so. "I've got something to feed your fantasies right here." He pulled her into straddling him on the couch, his cock a rock-hard advertisement for his intentions, even through the barrier of her skinny jeans.

She ground against him, making him groan. "But I'm not done with you yet."

"And you never will be." He slipped his hands under her t-shirt to lift it above her head, but she crossed her arms, not cooperating.

"I'm not convinced you're entirely healed, Kaden Grant." She had enough stubbornness in her arms folded across her chest that he knew at least part of that concern was real... and not just whatever game she was tormenting him with.

"I know one way to convince you." He practically launched her into the air by thrusting his hips up. She teetered forward, a grin on her face as her hands landed on his chest. That was more like it.

But she instantly got serious again. "Have you decided what to tell the mayor?"

Ah, so that was it.

"Yes," Kaden said, letting his voice drop. "I'm going to very politely and very sincerely tell him to fuck right off."

She smacked his chest.

He grinned.

"I'm serious," she said.

"So am I." He adjusted her position on top of him because it was clear they had to talk a bit first, and the way she was grinding on his cock, he would go off long before the main event. And that wasn't acceptable. In fact, this had to be absolutely the most perfect mating in the history of matings. Terra deserved no less.

"I know you want me to stay on the force, babe," he started, but she cut him off with a fast kiss that set his wolf humming.

"I want you to be happy," she said. "I just don't want you to give up being a police officer because of me."

"I'm not giving it up because of *you*," he said. "I'm giving it up because of *me*."

She scowled at him, but it was true.

The news of his white wolf shifting in front of half his division ran like wildfire through the department... along with the news that Julius McGovern, the mayor's personal friend, was in fact, the notorious Wolf Hunter. That news had rocked city hall until a few hours later when Julius McGovern was discovered dead in his home—he'd taken a bullet to the head *four days ago*. Right around the time that Terra first met with whoever had taken his place, posing as him in order to get close to the mayor's favorite artist.

That murder, plus the attempt on Terra's life, made the Wolf Hunter Public Enemy Number One in the Seattle Police Department. And the mayor had personally asked him to head the task force in charge of hunting the bastard down. As the first openly-shifter cop on the force, Kaden supposed it made sense. The mayor had even promised to implement a sweeping set of new policies in the department to ensure that shifters were welcome on the thin blue line that separated the criminal element from the law-abiding people of Seattle.

The only thing was... Kaden had other things to do.

He had a mate to claim. A pack to join. And a new life as a shifter, and possibly a witch, to discover. That single blue-energy bolt from his paw changed *everything* for him.

That, and the gorgeous woman who was staring into his eyes with great concern etched on her face.

He smoothed the crease on her brow. "I'm going take that job at Riverwise. I'm going to join my first pack and hunt down the Wolf Hunter with the help of the people who most want him caught. No matter what the mayor says, that's not the SPD. I can do more good at Riverwise. Plus there's this little matter of making sure my mate is safe at all times. That's not something I'll be able to do if I'm putting in face time at the office, trying to prove the SPD isn't anti-shifter by being their poster wolf."

Her shoulders dropped, but he also saw the hint of a smile and the glow on her face when he mentioned keeping her safe. It was important to her, he knew that, but he was dead serious about that—there was no fucking way he was leaving her with anyone else. And not just because the Wolf Hunter was still out there. Because she *belonged* to him.

And it was time to make that official.

"You're sure about this?" Terra asked one more time.

He took her cheeks in his hands and brought her down for a soft kiss. "Absolutely positive."

She nodded, and he could feel her approval through

the submission bond that bound them together. He was her alpha, and she trusted him to make the right decision. It flushed him with a literal magical energy that had his cock surging to attention again.

He slid his hands from her cheeks to her shirt. "I hope you're not fond of this." He shifted his hands to claws—they might not be as razor sharp as Noah's but they could easily slice through a cotton t-shirt. He shredded it as he pulled it apart at the neck, leaving Terra only in her flimsy bra.

She sucked in a breath, but he knew she liked it.

"The rest of it. Off. Now." He sliced away her bra, then shifted his hands back to human so he could cup those delicious breasts while her hands worked at the buttons on her pants. He lifted her off him and set her on the floor so she could wriggle out of them. He watched as she undressed for him, deliberately licking his lips like she had before. And because he was dying to taste her.

Her eyes hooded as her pants hit the floor.

He brought her back to straddling him on the couch. His cock was a flagpole now, ready for her in every way. "Ride me, Terra," he said hoarsely, but when she moved down toward his cock, he stopped her, his hands locked on her hips. "No. Up here." Then he slid under her until his face was directly below her sex.

She gasped as his tongue made the first kiss. Then she was quickly moaning and clutching at the couch as he worked her sensitive nub. He slipped his fingers in soon after, and in no time she was riding them, clutching his hair, urging him on. His girl was a hot one, wild in the sack every time and every way. It would be a challenge to keep coming up with new ways to take her to that peak and beyond, but he had a lifetime ahead of him to figure it all out.

Her moans turned to shrieks, and she quickly came, her body convulsing around his fingers and quivering against his tongue.

God damn, he liked making her come.

His cock was screaming to have her, and he wanted to save some for the main event, but he couldn't resist sliding forward before she could catch her breath and thrusting up deep inside her.

"Holy fuck," she whispered as he took her from beneath.

"Oh, yes it is," he gritted out between his teeth. She was so small and tight, it took him by surprise every damn time. He thrust up again, and soon she had the rhythm of it, bouncing down to meet him, driving him deeper and making him grunt with each stroke. His thumb found her nub again, the spot he'd just finished tormenting with his tongue, and her shrieks started climbing higher and higher.

The pleasure was grinding tight and low in his belly, but he wasn't letting it loose yet. He had more plans for this than two quick orgasms for her... but that was a damn fine place to start.

"Oh, God, Kaden!" she panted, head tipped back, praying his name as she bounced on his cock. He gave her nub the extra pressure it needed to rocket her over the edge. Her screams satisfied something male and primal and deep inside him, in a way even his own pleasure never could. She was *his*. She had surrendered to *him*. And she was floating on an ecstasy high because of it.

When her shrieks settled into pants again, he gripped her hips and slammed her hard down on his cock... and held her there. Then he curled up, staying buried deep, and held her close, one hand on the small of her back to keep her joined with him, the other at the back of her head to pull her in for a kiss. A soft, gentle kiss that spoke of all his tangled feelings for her—the worship, the love, the hot, tight feeling of need she brought out in him every moment he was near her.

"I want you," Kaden whispered against her lips.

"You *have* me," she replied, a little exasperated as if he couldn't have her any more deeply than he did at that moment.

Oh, but he could.

"I claim you for my mate, Terra Wilding," he breathed, his heart spilling out in his words. "I will make you mine. Forever."

She gasped, and her eyelids fluttered at the ancient words. They were primal, too, like all the feelings he had for her. He lifted her off his cock, instantly missing the feeling of her tight and warm around him, but he needed her on her hands and knees to do this right.

"Right now?" she gasped.

"Yes, right now," he said as he turned her in his lap and pressed her forward, so she would fall on her hands and knees, her beautiful rear-end enticingly up in the air. He bent over her, sweeping the hair from where it cascaded over her back and whispering, "Now and always. You are *mine.*"

Then he took her from behind, the way he'd been dreaming of from the start.

Kaden filled her, hard and fast.

He seemed to know just how she liked it, even when she didn't know herself.

His control loosened, and she felt his grunts as much as heard them, through the pounding of his cock and the hard grip of his hands on her hips. He'd already brought her to climax twice, but every part of her was quivering with anticipation. Would he take her this time, truly take her as a mate?

Her pleasure ramped up as he slid forward, winding his fingers in her hair, gripping it hard and pulling her head back. A minute ago, she was riding him like the world's most decadent horse, but now he was riding her... *hard*... and it was hotter than anything she'd ever felt. His rock-hard cock was owning her. His strong hands were commanding her. And soon enough, his hard-breathing grunts leaned down toward her exposed neck, his fangs out and grazing her flesh.

Oh God yes.

His thrusts gained even more power, racing her toward a climax that was going to shatter everything that she was—break her apart so she could be put back together as a new woman.

A mated female.

With the strongest alpha she had ever met.

"You are *mine.*" The words were barely out of his mouth before he sank his fangs into her. The pain shoved her right over the edge, the climax rippling through and whiting out any and all thoughts she had beyond the pulsing pleasure in her body and the searing heat of his magic. It started as twin fountains of burning hot pleasure—one between her legs, the other where his fangs had clamped onto her flesh—and it quickly spread throughout her body, setting her on fire and flushing her with more pleasure than she'd ever known. He was still riding her, still pumping her, but when the magic filtered through every cell in her body, turning her more fully alive than she'd ever been, he reached his climax and roared through his bite, still buried deep and pulsing inside her. She felt his seed fill her and wished for a moment that she actually had been fertile at that moment… so she could start building a family with this magnificent man and beast.

Kaden stayed deep inside her through his climax, then released her from his bite.

His breathing was so ragged, he didn't speak, just pulled out of her, then pulled her back to his chest, bringing her with him as he rocked back and lay down prone on the couch again.

"God, I hope we can do that every fucking day," he breathed out. "Every day, Terra. You understand? We're doing that every day."

She couldn't smile any harder as she curled up against his still-heaving chest.

"I might have to start exercising or something to build up endurance."

"Do what you like, babe," he said, still breathless, but now his hands were roaming her. "But I plan to work that sweet little body of yours hard *every damn day*. The bite included because *Jesus Fucking Christ* that was good."

She crawled up to face him. His magic was singing through her body, binding her to him in a way so complete, she wasn't even sure where she ended and he began. It was stronger than any submission bond. Stronger than anything she'd ever felt. And with Kaden's magic wrapping her in a warm blanket of his love, she knew that she would always be safe.

The darkness of her life had been permanently banished.

She lightly kissed him on the lips. He grabbed hold of her and kissed her thoroughly.

"You're lucky a man needs a certain amount of time to recover," he said, a gleam in his eye. "Or I'd be making you scream all over again right this moment."

"I'm ready anytime you are, my sexy beast." She grinned at him.

His eyes flashed. "Just one of the many things I love about you."

Her heart stuttered for a moment. It could have been the magic that was coursing through every vein of her body… or it could have been *that word*.

He grinned and quickly rolled her to reverse their positions on the couch. His massively muscled body was now on top of her—not crushing her, but definitely dominating her tiny-by-comparison form. And there was an unmistakable growing hardness prodding her leg.

Her eyes went wide. "Already?"

"With you… always." He reached a strong hand between her legs, making her jump when he pressed on her nub, still swollen and sensitive with the mind-blowing sex and the magical rush of his bite. Then he spread her legs, bringing one up around his back. His already-stiff cock was pressing again at her entrance. He pulled back and then entered her with one swift stroke.

She arched up and gasped. She hadn't thought she

could want more, or that her body could even take any more pleasure, but apparently it could.

With Kaden, it always would.

He took her with slow, long strokes, and she could tell this time would be different. Longer, slower, more intense... and just the beginning of everything they would share.

He pulled in a breath with each thrust and then said, "Always," on each release, over and over again. Her heart soared higher with each one.

She would never have enough.

CHAPTER 17

It had taken Terra three weeks, but the *People of Seattle* exhibit was finally ready.

"It's absolutely stunning!" Sally proclaimed.

Terra was proud of her work—she wouldn't show it, if she weren't—but she was pretty sure Sally's exuberance was related at least partially to the massive influx of people into her gallery to see the first exhibit of shifter art. The pictures she had taken of the wolves in her cousin Marco's gang filled Sally's walls and spoke to

Terra's heart. That so many people wanted to see the images first-hand was filling Terra with light—*this* was the heart of her city. This was the part that was open and caring and wanted to embrace the wolves in their midst, not cower in fear from them.

Riverwise security was thick amongst the crowd—Kaden had insisted on twice the number as at her last exhibit—but Terra felt in her heart that, on this day at least, the light was winning.

Her mate never let her out of his sight, which felt like a warm blanket holding her secure, but he must have finished checking in with his crew, because he was cruising over to her, grabbing a flute of champagne off a passing platter to bring to her.

Sally saw him coming and decided to make her exit gracefully. "I think I see the mayor!" she squealed and ran off.

Terra chuckled, then squinted at the Sally and the mayor, wondering if she had talked him into her bed. He had been newly widowed just a few years ago, and Terra would be surprised if Sally hadn't at least tried.

Kaden arrived at her side, kissed her, and handed her the drink. Given she was standing in a room surrounded by her art as well, Terra figured this was as close to heaven as she would get... outside their bedroom at the Riverwise estate.

Which was something she wanted to discuss with Kaden as well.

"You're a hit," Kaden said softly, the pride in his voice making her heart swell.

"They're the stars," she said, gesturing with her glass to the images of the wolves, young and old, that she had framed on the wall. "I just captured their light."

Kaden smiled wide. She had taken dozens of pictures of him, trying to capture his light, but the real thing would always outshine them.

She ducked her head. "I want to build us a home," she said softly, not sure why she just blurted these things out at the least opportune times.

"A home?" he asked, his eyebrows lifting. "As in a house with four walls?"

She nodded, then peered up at him. "I want to build it next to the River estate. I want a sunroom and a darkroom... and a nursery." She bit her lip. This was only part of her plan, but it was the key part. They were mated but not married. Kaden still kept his apartment in the city, even though they'd been effectively living a honeymoon life at the River estate at Mama River's insistence.

Kaden seemed to struggle for a moment to speak. Then he cleared his throat. "Well, it's a good thing I picked up this ring today."

Her eyes flew wide as he dropped to one knee and fished a small box out of the pocket of his Riverwise jacket. A whisper went around the room, and heads turned, but all she could see was the glittering sapphire-and-gold band Kaden was holding up to her.

"Would you do me the honor of becoming my wife?" Kaden asked, voice deep and booming in the sudden silence of the gallery.

Tears sprung to her eyes. "Yes," she whispered, but it must have carried because a round of applause went up around the room. She threw her arms around Kaden, and he rose to hold her, which was good because her legs were suddenly unsteady. He slipped the ring on her finger while her mouth was still trying to find words to say how happy he had just made her.

She gave up and just kissed him instead.

When they broke apart, the crowd seemed to have gone back to the art... except her brother and sister were staring at her from a dozen feet away. Cassie's face was lit up with the widest smile Terra had ever seen on her, but

Trent looked like he'd just been hit by a bus but hadn't figured it out yet—dazed and confused.

Terra held an arm out to Cassie, and she skittered across the gallery floor to hug her tight.

Then she peered up at Terra. "I want to be the flower girl!" she said.

"Flower girl?" Terra pretended to be aghast. "You're my maid of honor. Of course."

"*And* the flower girl," Cassie insisted with an impish look.

"We can make that work, short stuff," Kaden said, a smirk on his face as he ruffled her hair.

Cassie looked like *she* wanted to be the one marrying Kaden, and Terra couldn't blame her a bit.

Trent finally arrived at their little circle. He awkwardly held his hand out to Kaden. "Well, I guess congratulations are in order."

Kaden shook his hand but didn't say anything.

Trent turned to her. "And… I guess this means you'll be moving out of the River estate?" There wasn't quite disapproval in his voice, but there wasn't approval, either. It was the kind of vague thing her father would say, and it made Terra's stomach twist.

She held in her sigh. "Actually, that's something I

wanted to discuss with you." And by *discuss*, she meant *inform*, because Trent wasn't going to have a vote on this, either. "I'm going to use my trust fund to build a home next to the River family estate. There's some property for sale there. But I'm also going to help Mama River out with some modifications to the River estate itself. I want to expand it. Reinforce it. Make it secure. I'm really just building upon her vision—I want there to always be a safe refuge for shifters there."

Trent's eyebrows raised up and stayed up. "That's... an interesting idea."

"The location of the estate is already known to the public," Terra went on, ignoring the disapproval in his voice. "It's *out*... just like our family. But there are still hard times ahead for every shifter in the city." She swept her hand out to include all the wolves in her exhibit as well as beyond the walls. "I want them to know there's a place they can come and be accepted."

Trent was struggling for something to say.

"It's an amazing idea, Terra." Kaden gave her a kiss on the cheek and draped his arm protectively over her shoulder. It meant the world to her, especially since she hadn't given him any notice whatsoever about this. She'd only pulled the idea together with Mama River this morning, and she had planned to tell Kaden after the show.

"Can I come live with Mama River again?" Cassie asked brightly.

Terra grinned. "She would love that. But you have school now, right?"

Her face scrunched up. "Yeah, I guess so."

"We'll talk about it later," Terra said, but either way was fine with her. Wherever Cassie wanted to be, that's where she should go. Terra was building her own life now, but her family would always be part of it. "However, you can visit me and Kaden in our new home whenever you like."

That brightened her smile again.

"Is this really safe?" Trent finally managed to ask. He seemed to direct the question as much to Kaden as to Terra.

"We'll make it safe," Kaden said, and Terra had no doubt that would be true.

"We have to take a stand somewhere, Trent," Terra added. "I'm not letting someone like the Wolf Hunter decide how I'm going to live my life. Not anymore." She was echoing Mama River in that, but the woman was a pillar of strength, and it was an honor to follow in her footsteps.

Trent's eyes widened a little. Then he gave just the barest of nods. But it was approval, and it made Terra's heart sing.

A murmur went up through the crowd at the gallery. Kaden frowned and checked in with his earpiece—then he frowned even more.

"Is something wrong?" Terra asked. Was her newfound bravery in the face of the Wolf Hunter threat going to be tested so soon? People around the gallery were pulling out their phones and huddling together in groups.

"The gallery is secure," Kaden said, still listening to his earpiece. "But you might want to check the news."

Trent had his phone out first, and his frown turned quickly into a scowl. "There's a new Wolf Hunter video." He held the small screen out for everyone to see.

As it started, all Terra could think was, *Of course he did*—the Wolf Hunter ran right out and made another video, just so she would know he had survived. Her determination to carry out her plans only strengthened as she watched him spew his hatred on the video.

"We have to rid the city of this scourge!" he was saying, back in his mask, but she knew that body. She knew those cold, blue eyes.

"That's him," she said softly.

Kaden looked to her. "Julius?"

She nodded. Although that wasn't his name, of course.

Then an image on the video caught her attention again—*it was hers.* One of the photos she had taken while at Marco's headquarters. The grandmotherly wolf stared out from the video as the Wolf Hunter's voice boomed hate over it.

"This isn't just about a certain high-profile wolf," the voice said. "This isn't just about one or two packs. This menace breeds in the underground of our city! And the only way to stamp it out is to take the fight to the streets, where they live!"

Terra's throat tightened. *The streets.* He's talking about the shifter gangs. Marco's gang. And her photographs led the Wolf Hunter right to them.

"Join me, crusaders!" the Wolf Hunter shouted from the phone. "Join our militia! Join the war to bring humanity back to the top of the food chain! And help me eliminate this shifter threat before they spread their demon seeds any deeper into the DNA of our city!"

The video ended, and Terra shuddered.

She turned to her brother. "I want to get started building reinforcements for the River estate right away."

He nodded his agreement, and after a slight hesitation, he came over to give her a hug. "You're a stronger wolf than I'll ever be, sis," he whispered, low enough for only her to hear.

"We're all stronger when we stand together," she said.

The days ahead would surely put that idea to the test.

Want more Wilding Pack?
WILD ONE (Wilding Pack Wolves 4)

**He's a shifter gang leader.
She's a halfling on the run.
And the Wolf Hunter has just declared open
season on them both.**
Get WILD ONE today!

Subscribe to Alisa's newsletter to know when a new book
is coming out!
http://smarturl.it/AlphaLoversNews

ABOUT THE AUTHOR

Alisa Woods lives in the Midwest with her husband and family, but her heart will always belong to the beaches and mountains where she grew up. She writes sexy paranormal romances about alpha men and the women who love them. She enjoys exploring the struggles we all have, where we resist—and succumb to—our most tempting vices as well as our greatest desires. She firmly believes that love triumphs over all.

All of Alisa's romances feature sexy alphas and the strong women who love them.

23825059R00155

Printed in Poland
by Amazon Fulfillment
Poland Sp. z o.o., Wrocław